"THE COMING OF THE AVENGERS!"

THE FIRST OF A STAR-STUDDED SERIES *of* **BOOK-LENGTH SUPER-EPICS** *featuring some of* **EARTH'S GREATEST SUPER-HEROES!**

The MIGHTY THOR

IRON-MAN

ANT-MAN and the WASP

The Incredible HULK

THE PLACE: ASGARD, HOME OF THE NORSE GODS!
THE TIME: THE PRESENT!
THE MAN: LOKI, GOD OF EVIL! A PRISONER ON THE DREADED *ISLE OF SILENCE*...PLOTTING AWESOME REVENGE AGAINST HIS MIGHTY ENEMY, *THOR*, THE THUNDER GOD!

| WRITTEN BY: STAN LEE | DRAWN BY: JACK KIRBY | INKING: DICK AYERS | LETTERING: S. ROSEN |

2

IT IS BECAUSE OF THE ACCURSED *THOR* THAT I AM EXILED TO THIS BARREN ISLE, ORDERED TO *REMAIN* HERE BY *ODIN,* KING OF THE GODS!

BUT THOUGH MY *BODY* MAY BE IMPRISONED, *NONE* CAN STOP MY MAGIC *POWERS* FROM ROAMING THE UNIVERSE IN SEARCH OF *REVENGE!*

BY MEANS OF *THOUGHT PROJECTION* I SHALL SEND MY DISEMBODIED SELF PAST THE RAINBOW BRIDGE DOWN TO EARTH! THERE I SHALL FIND SOME WAY TO MAKE *THOR* COME BACK TO ASGARD, WHERE I CAN BATTLE HIM AGAIN, AND *DEFEAT* HIM FOREVER!

THERE HE IS, IN HIS HUMAN IDENTITY AS *DR. DON BLAKE,* LAME, MILD-MANNERED TREATER OF THE SICK AND INJURED!

S'LONG, DOC! I FEEL LOTS BETTER NOW!

HIT A FEW HOMERS IN TODAY'S GAME FOR ME, BOBBY!

BAH! DEFEATING DON BLAKE MEANS *NOTHING* TO ME! IT WOULD BE A HOLLOW VICTORY!

ONLY BY CONQUERING HIM AS *THOR* WILL MY REVENGE BE COMPLETE! BUT IT WILL REQUIRE A FEARFUL MENACE TO MAKE THE DULL DOCTOR BECOME THE MIGHTY THUNDER GOD! I MUST SCAN EARTH TILL I *FIND* SUCH A MENACE!

AFTER LONG HOURS OF SUPER-NATURAL OBSERVATION, *LOKI* FINDS...

A HUGE HUMAN FIGURE... FLYING THROUGH THE AIR! HOW IS IT POSSIBLE?

NO...HE IS *NOT* FLYING! HE IS COVERING THE AREA IN FANTASTIC, POWERFUL *LEAPS!* NOW I SEE! IT IS THE INCREDIBLE *HULK!!*

2.

3

ALTHOUGH THERE IS NO EVIL IN HIS HEART, MANKIND *FEARS* HIM BECAUSE OF HIS AWESOME STRENGTH! *HE* SHALL BE THE PERFECT FOIL FOR ME!

BUT, WHAT DIABOLICAL SCHEME SHALL I EMPLOY? AH, I HAVE IT! THAT *RAILROAD TRESTLE!*

ALL I NEED DO IS PROJECT A MENTAL IMAGE UPON THE TRACKS, WHERE THE *HULK* WILL SEE IT!

THERE, IT IS DONE! THE WITLESS MORTAL WILL THINK HE SEES A REAL BUNDLE OF TNT, ABOUT TO DESTROY THE TRESTLE JUST AS THE TRAIN IS APPROACHING!

PERFECT! HE *SEES* IT! AND NOW, NOT DREAMING IT IS ONLY A NON-EXISTENT IMAGE, HE LEAPS DOWN TO SNUFF IT OUT BEFORE IT CAN EXPLODE!

BUT THERE IS *NO* TNT, AND SO, REACHING FOR SOMETHING THAT IS NOT THERE, HE MISCALCULATES THE FORCE OF HIS PLUNGE, CRASHING INTO THE TRESTLE, AND *SHATTERING* IT!

CHARLIE! STOP THE TRAIN! SOMETHING SMASHED THE TRESTLE UP AHEAD! WE'LL *CRASH!*

IMPOSSIBLE!! WE'RE GOING TOO FAST! WE'LL *NEVER* STOP IN TIME!

HAH! IT WORKED JUST AS I PLANNED! WHEN THE TRAIN CRASHES, THE *HULK* WILL BE BLAMED! HE WILL BECOME THE MOST WANTED MAN ON EARTH! DR. BLAKE IS CERTAIN TO BECOME *THOR* TO JOIN IN THE HUNT... LITTLE DREAMING THAT THAT IS JUST WHAT *LOKI* WANTS! BUT, *WAIT!* WHY IS THE *HULK* CARRYING THAT HUGE BOULDER?

HE HAS PLACED IT UNDER THE TRACKS!...IS USING IT AS A SUPPORT, TO STAND ON! THE *FOOL!* WHAT GOOD WILL *THAT* DO? THE TRAIN IS ALMOST UPON HIM!

3.

LOOK! THAT HEAD JUTTING THROUGH THE TRACKS!

IT'S THE *HULK!* HE DID THIS! HE'S TRYING TO KILL US ALL! I--I CAN'T STOP IN TIME!

BUT, USING THE ALMOST LIMITLESS STRENGTH OF HIS INCREDIBLE BODY, THE *HULK* BENDS BELOW THE TRACKS, SUPPORTING THEM WITH HIS MASSIVE BACK, AS THE TRAIN PASSES SAFELY BY...

BUT THEN...

ALL SAFE! ..CAN'T HOLD ANY LONGER...

WHOOSH!

CRASH!

HE SAVED THE TRAIN, BUT ONLY *I* KNOW THAT! THE HUMANS WILL STILL THINK HE TRIED TO SLAY THEM...THE HUNT WILL BE ON! AND *THOR* WILL LIVE AGAIN!....ALL BECAUSE OF *LOKI*, THE MASTER SCHEMER!

HOURS LATER, AS *LOKI* PREDICTED...

BETTER LOCK YOUR DOORS, BOYS! THE *HULK'S* ON THE RAMPAGE AGAIN!

A LOT OF GOOD LOCKING A DOOR WILL DO AGAINST *THAT* GORILLA!

HULK IN ATTACK ON TRAIN!

NATION SHOCKED! ARMY TO MOBILIZE!

THEN, THE ONE LIVING BEING WHO KNOWS THE TRUTH ABOUT THE *HULK* READS THE REPORT IN AMAZEMENT!

IT *CAN'T* BE! HE'D *NEVER* DO A THING LIKE THAT!...NO MATTER *WHAT!!*

OR..OR *WOULD* HE?

CITY NEWS

TRAIN ENGINEER IDENTIFIES HULK AS WOULD-BE WRECKER!

HUL IN ATT ON TRA

WITHIN MINUTES, *RICK JONES* SUMMONS MEMBERS OF HIS NEWLY FORMED *TEEN BRIGADE** A GROUP OF YOUTHFUL RADIO HAM ENTHUSIASTS...

IF THE *HULK* IS INNOCENT, HE NEEDS HELP, FAST! AND IF HE'S GUILTY, IT'LL TAKE MORE THAN THE *ARMY* TO STOP 'IM!

WE'VE GOTTA CONTACT SOMEONE WITH EQUAL POWERS...LIKE THE *FANTASTIC FOUR!*

*TEEN BRIGADE FORMED IN ISSUE OF *HULK* #6.

DON'T JUST SIT THERE, FELLA! START SENDING! USE THE *FF'S* SPECIAL WAVELENGTH! TELL 'EM TO CONTACT ME, *PRONTO*, BEFORE ANY INNOCENT JOKERS GET HURT REAL BAD!

YOU HEARD THE MAN, WILLIE! NOW *MOVE!*

AND SO, SECONDS LATER, A FRANTIC MESSAGE IS BEAMED FROM THE HEADQUARTERS OF THE *TEEN BRIGADE*, IN THE SOUTHWEST, HALFWAY ACROSS THE COUNTRY TOWARDS NEW YORK!

CALLING THE *FANTASTIC FOUR!* CONDITION *RED!* CONTACT *TEEN BRIGADE!!* *HULK* MUST BE FOUND!! DO YOU READ ME?

4.

BUT THE SINISTER GOD OF EVIL HAS *OTHER* PLANS...

THE *FANTASTIC FOUR* WILL RUIN EVERYTHING! IT IS *THOR* I WANT!...NO ONE ELSE! I MUST TAKE INSTANT ACTION!

THERE! I HAVE USED MY MENTAL POWERS TO JAM THE RADIO WAVES, DIVERTING THEM TO A DIFFERENT WAVE-LENGTH...ONE WHICH I KNOW *DON BLAKE* IS LISTENING TO!

AND, IN THE QUIET STUDY OF DR. BLAKE...

...CONTACT *TEEN BRIGADE!* HULK MUST BE FOUND! DO YOU READ US?

STRANGE! SOUNDS LIKE A CALL FOR *THOR!*

THE *TEEN BRIGADE!* THEY'RE LOCATED IN THE SOUTH-WEST! IF THIS CONCERNS THE *HULK*, IT MUST BE SERIOUS! AND SO, THE TIME HAS COME...

...FOR DR. DON BLAKE TO STRIKE HIS ENCHANTED CANE ONCE UPON THE FLOOR, CASTING OFF HIS MORTAL GUISE, AND BECOMING...

...THE MIGHTY *THOR*, GOD OF *THUNDER!*

BUT, UNSUSPECTED BY *LOKI*, OTHERS HAVE *ALSO* HEARD THE RADIO MESSAGE, AND THOUGHT IT WAS BEAMED TO THEM! AMONG THEM ARE THE ASTONISHING *ANT-MAN* AND THE *WASP!*

WAIT FOR *ME, ANT-MAN!*

I THOUGHT YOU WEREN'T COMING, JAN!

I CAN'T SEE WHY YOU HAVE TO STOP AND POWDER YOUR NOSE EVERY TIME WE HAVE A MISSION!

HENRY PYM, YOU'RE BEGINNING TO SOUND LIKE A STUFFY OLD *BACHELOR* AGAIN!

AND I INTEND TO *REMAIN* THAT WAY! NOW SEE IF YOU CAN'T BE QUIET LONG ENOUGH FOR ME TO ACTIVATE THE DOUBLE CATAPULT!

BUT WHY DO *I* HAVE TO USE YOUR SILLY FLYING ANT RELAYS? I HAPPEN TO HAVE MY *OWN* WINGS!

BUT WE'VE GOT A *THOUSAND* MILES TO COVER, JAN, AND I DON'T WANT YOU EXHAUSTED WHEN WE GET THERE!

6

AND STILL *ANOTHER* PAIR OF EARS HAVE INTERCEPTED THE URGENT BROAD-CAST...THE EARS OF *ANTHONY STARK*, MILLIONAIRE INDUSTRIALIST AND PLAYBOY...BETTER KNOWN TO THE UNSUSPECTING WORLD AS *IRON MAN!*

LUCKY I WAS TUNED IN TO THE RIGHT FREQUENCY! THINGS HAVE BEEN TOO DULL AROUND HERE LATELY!

I'VE ALWAYS *WONDERED* WHETHER THE *HULK* REALLY EXISTED, AND WHETHER *IRON MAN'S* STRENGTH WAS A MATCH FOR HIM!

LOOKS AS THOUGH I'LL GET A CHANCE TO FIND OUT! SOONER THAN I THOUGHT!

I'LL PROPEL MYSELF FOR MOST OF THE TRIP BY MY SOLAR BATTERY! IT'S SLOWER THAN MY TRANSISTORS, BUT IT LASTS LONGER... AND I'VE GOT A LONG WAY TO GO!

THEN, AFTER A FEW HOURS OF CROSS-COUNTRY FLYING...

ALMOST THERE! NOW TO SWITCH TO MY TRANSISTORS BEFORE I LULL MYSELF TO SLEEP UP HERE!

AHHH! THIS IS MORE *LIKE* IT!

MEANWHILE, IN THE MAIN CLUBROOM OF THE *TEEN BRIGADE*, A FEELING OF *GLOOM* FILLS THE AIR...

STILL NO WORD FROM THE FF, EH?

GUESS THEY NEVER GOT THE MESSAGE!

OR ELSE THEY CAN'T BE BOTHERED TO ANSWER A BUNCH OF KIDS LIKE US!

HEY! HOLD IT, YOU GUYS! *CLAM UP!* I'M GETTIN' SOMETHIN'...IT...IT'S *MR. FANTASTIC!*

WELL, C'MON, RICK... *GIVE!!* WHAT DOES HE *SAY?* LET US IN ON IT!!

WE'VE JUST INTERCEPTED A MESSAGE FROM YOU, RICK! IT WAS BROAD-CAST ON THE WRONG WAVELENGTH SOMEHOW!

PHOOEY! EVERY-TIME THERE'S SOME-THIN' HEAVY TO BE LIFTED AROUND HERE, OL' PRETTY BOY GETS A CALL ON THAT BLASTED RADIO!

BEN GRIMM! YOU KNOW YOU GET MIKE FRIGHT EVERY TIME *YOU* HAVE TO USE IT!

6.

7

BUT, BACK IN ASGARD...

BAH! THIS COMPLICATES THINGS FOR ME! I ONLY WANT TO FIND A WAY TO LURE THOR UP HERE! I AM NOT INTERESTED IN THOSE OTHERS!

THOR IS AT THE WINDOW NOW! IF I MOVE QUICKLY, I MAY STILL SUCCEED! I'LL CREATE A MENTAL IMAGE OF THE HULK AND MAKE IT RUN PAST THOR'S FIELD OF VISION!

I THOUGHT I SAW... IT IS! IT'S THE HULK!

NO NEED FOR ME TO DISTURB THE OTHERS!

NO MATTER HOW FAST HE CAN LEAP, I ALWAYS FOLLOW HIM!...

...BY HURLING MY MIGHTY HAMMER AND HOLDING ONTO THE UNBREAKABLE THONG!

STRANGE! HE MOVES AS THOUGH HE HASN'T SEEN ME...AS THOUGH HE IS UNAWARE OF ANYTHING!

NO! NOW HE SEES ME! HE IS GRASPING THAT HUGE BOULDER! HE INTENDS TO HURL IT AT ME! BUT MY HAMMER WILL STOP HIM!

IMPOSSIBLE! IT... IT WENT RIGHT THROUGH HIM!

NOW HE'S FADING AWAY! IT ISN'T THE HULK AT ALL! MERELY A MENTAL IMAGE!

ONLY LOKI IS CAPABLE OF SUCH WIZARDRY! I SHOULD HAVE SUSPECTED! HE MUST BE BEHIND IT!

8.

LOKI, THOU EVIL ONE! I KNOW NOT WHAT YOUR PLAN IS, BUT I HAVE WARNED YOU NEVER TO MEDDLE IN EARTH AFFAIRS! AND NOW YOU DARE DEFY ME!

I HAVE SUCCEEDED! HE IS RETURNING TO ASGARD! BUT WHEN HE REACHES THE ISLE OF SILENCE, IT IS I WHO SHALL EMERGE THE VICTOR!... FOR THIS TIME I AM READY FOR THE COMING OF THOR!

BUT, BACK ON EARTH, THE WHEELS SET IN MOTION BY VILLAINOUS LOKI CANNOT BE STOPPED! THE HULK IS STILL AT LARGE... AND OUR AMAZING SAGA HAS BARELY BEGUN!

THOR HAS DISAPPEARED! BUT DON'T WORRY, LAD!... I'M SURE THAT ANT-MAN AND I WILL BE ABLE TO FIND THE HULK AND TO LEARN THE TRUTH!

IF HE REALLY IS ON A RAMPAGE, LOOK OUT!! HE'S STRONGER THAN ANY-ONE EVEN SUSPECTS! BUT IF HE'S INNOCENT, HE MUST NOT BE HURT... UNDER-STAND?

MEANWHILE, WHERE IS THE INCREDIBLE HULK? HUNTED, HOUNDED, BEWILDERED, HE HAS TAKEN REFUGE WITH A TRAVELING CIRCUS, AS HE WONDERS WHAT TO DO NEXT!

THERE HE IS LADIES AND GENTLEMEN... MECHANO, THE MOST POWERFUL, LIFELIKE ROBOT ON EARTH! HE WALKS LIKE A MAN, HE MOVES LIKE A MAN, BUT HE IS AS STRONG AS A DOZEN BULLDOZERS! MECHANO, THE MARVEL OF THE AGE!!

9.

11

MEANWHILE, THE AUDIENCE, THINKING IT IS ALL PART OF THE SHOW, HOWLS WITH UNRESTRAINED ENTHUSIASM...

BEST DURN ACT I EVER SAW!

THAT BIG ROBOT HAS THE DISPOSITION OF MY BROTHER-IN-LAW!

HOW DO THEY EVER DREAM THESE THINGS UP?

SO! YOU REFUSE TO STOP??

YOU INTEND TO KEEP HOUNDING ME, DO YOU?

ALL RIGHT, THE MASQUERADE'S OVER! I DON'T CARE WHO KNOWS WHO I AM! SOON AS I WIPE THIS STUPID MAKE-UP OFF, I'M GONNA RIP THIS PLACE APART WITH MY BARE HANDS! WHAT HAVE I GOT TO FEAR! NOTHING CAN HURT THE HULK!

THEN, AS THE STARTLED, INCREDULOUS AUDIENCE RECOILS IN PANIC...

WE'VE DONE IT! WE'VE BROUGHT HIM OUT INTO THE OPEN! NOW EVERY SECOND COUNTS! LURE HIM UNDER THE TRAPEZE NET! I'LL DO THE REST!

DON'T LET ME DOWN, HENRY! I WOULDN'T WANT HIM FOR A PERMANENT PLAYMATE!

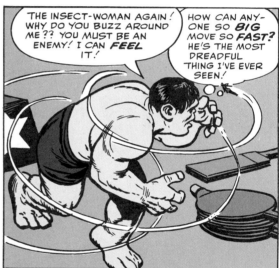

THE INSECT-WOMAN AGAIN! WHY DO YOU BUZZ AROUND ME?? YOU MUST BE AN ENEMY! I CAN FEEL IT!

HOW CAN ANYONE SO BIG MOVE SO FAST? HE'S THE MOST DREADFUL THING I'VE EVER SEEN!

YOU THINK YOU CAN ESCAPE ME BECAUSE OF YOUR SIZE? NO ONE ESCAPES THE HULK!

OHHH...

THAT BELLOWS! FEELS LIKE A HURRICANE! ¡GASP!¿ CAN'T BREATHE! CAN'T SEE...OUT OF CONTROL! HENRY... HELP!!

NO ONE CAN SAVE YOU NOW!

12.

SUDDENLY, A MASSIVE GOLDEN FIGURE BREAKS THROUGH THE CROWD OF AMAZED SPECTATORS, AND THE SHOCK OF SEEING *IRON MAN* CHARGING TOWARDS HIM MAKES THE *HULK* TEMPORARILY FORGET HIS TINY PRISONER!

YOU'RE *WRONG!* THERE IS *ONE* WHO CAN SAVE HER!

IRON MAN!

THROUGH HIS TRANSISTOR-POWERED, BUILT-IN RADIO RECEIVER, THE GOLDEN WARRIOR HEARS A TERSE REPORT FROM NEARBY *ANT-MAN!*

PERFECT TIMING, *IRON MAN!* NOW, QUICKLY...MAKE HIM RUN TOWARD THE CENTER OF THE ARENA! I'VE PREPARED A TRAP FOR HIM! LET HIM TRY TO ESCAPE BY LEAPING THROUGH THE TOP OF THE TENT!

AND, AS THE *HULK* EXECUTES ONE OF HIS INCREDIBLE LEAPS, CRASHING THROUGH THE VERY TOP OF THE CIRCUS TENT...

ARGHH!

HE HIT THE SPECIAL NYLON SAFETY NETTING WHICH MY ANTS SPREAD OVER THE TOP OF THE TENT! NOW IF IT WILL ONLY HOLD HIM LONG ENOUGH!

BUT CAN ANY MERE NYLON NETTING BE STRONG ENOUGH TO HOLD THE RAMPAGING, EXPLODING HUMAN POWERHOUSE THAT IS THE *HULK?* WITH A MIGHTY SURGE OF BRUTE FORCE HE HURLS HIMSELF UPWARD, TAKING ALL THE NETTING AND THE ENTIRE TENT WITH HIM!

HE'S GETTING *AWAY!!*

NEVER HAVE HUMAN EYES BEHELD SUCH AN AWESOME SPECTACLE...NEVER HAS MORTAL MAN WITNESSED SUCH A STUPENDOUS SIGHT.!!

SECONDS LATER, HAVING RIPPED OFF THE ENTANGLING FABRICS ON THE SHAGGY PEAKS NEARBY, THE *HULK* CONTINUES HIS FRENZIED FLIGHT... WITH A LONE PURSUER!

THERE IS NO PLACE ON EARTH WHERE I CANNOT FOLLOW YOU!

13.

SUDDENLY, THE MIGHTY FUGITIVE DROPS TO EARTH, AS HIS GOLDEN PURSUER, UNABLE TO STOP IN TIME, WHIZZES OVER HIM!

THEN, WITH THE SPEED OF A CHARGING DREADNOUGHT, THE *HULK* LEAPS INTO THE AIR AGAIN, BEHIND THE STARTLED *IRON MAN!*

IN A TRICE THE HUNTED HAS BECOME THE HUNTER, AS A THUNDEROUS BLOW TO HIS POWER-PACK DAMAGES *IRON MAN'S* PROPULSION BATTERY!

NO ONE CAN STOP THE *HULK!*

CAN'T GO AFTER HIM TILL I REPAIR MY BATTERY!

HULK... WAIT! I WANT TO *HELP* YOU! TRUST ME! YOU CAN'T REMAIN A FUGITIVE *FOREVER!* COME BACK!!

BAH! I DON'T TRUST *ANYBODY!*

MEANWHILE, WHAT OF THE MIGHTY *THOR?* AT THAT MOMENT, IN THE GRAND CHAMBER OF THE IMPERIAL PALACE AT ASGARD...

NOBLE ODIN, LORD OF GODS! GRANT THY SON PERMISSION TO VISIT *LOKI* ON THE ISLE OF SILENCE, THAT I MAY LEARN IF HE IS RESPONSIBLE FOR SOME DEVILTRY ON EARTH!

WE GRANT THEE PERMISSION, BELOVED *THOR!* BUT HARK TO THESE WORDS...

THOUGH *YOU* BE THE SON OF MY HEART..*LOKI* TOO IS MY SON! I CANNOT INTERFERE IN WHAT TRANSPIRES BETWEEN YOU!

I UNDERSTAND, FATHER!

AND SO, ALONE IN THE NIGHT, THE MIGHTY THUNDER-GOD SETS OUT ACROSS THE SEA OF MIST... AWARE THAT THE ENEMY HE SEEKS IS ALSO A LEGENDARY GOD...AND THE MOST SINISTER, THE MOST DANGEROUS OF ALL!

LOKI MUST KNOW I AM COMING! HE MUST HAVE SET MANY TRAPS FOR ME! BUT I DARE NOT TURN BACK ...NO MATTER WHAT THE RISK!

14.

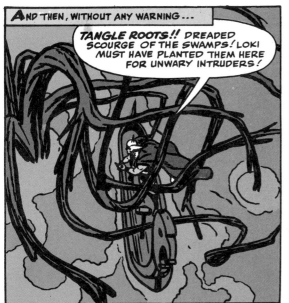

THE ISLE IS DIRECTLY AHEAD! LUCKILY MY LUNGS ARE STRONG...IF I CAN JUST HOLD MY BREATH FOR ANOTHER FEW MINUTES!

AND, ON SHORE, A GLOATING FIGURE SURVEYS THE NOW-SILENT SEA...

HIS CRAFT IS EMPTY! HE IS NOWHERE TO BE SEEN! HAVE I DEFEATED HIM SO SOON?!

THEN, AS IF IN ANSWER TO LOKI'S WORDS, A GIGANTIC WATER-SPOUT SHOOTS INTO THE AIR...AND...

NO, EVIL BROTHER! THE BATTLE HAS YET TO BEGIN!

HAVE YOU FORGOTTEN MY HAMMER IS CAPABLE OF CREATING WATER-SPOUTS, AS WELL AS PUNISHING MY FOES!?

WITH THE SPEED OF THOUGHT, LOKI FREEZES THE MOLECULES IN THE AIR, CREATING AN ICY SHIELD, JUST STRONG ENOUGH TO DEFLECT THOR'S HAMMER!

HAH! I AM TOO FAST FOR YOU!

YOU WERE EXPECTING ME, LOKI! THAT MEANS YOU HAVE COMMITTED SOME FOUL DEED, KNOWING I WOULD COME TO AVENGE IT!

AND AVENGE IT I SHALL!!

NOTHING CAN SAVE YOU FROM ME NOW, PRINCE OF EVIL!

STOP, ACCURSED BROTHER! DO YOU REMEMBER THE NAME OF THIS ISLE...AND THE ONES FOR WHOM IT WAS NAMED?

THE SILENT ONES, WHO LIVE BELOW! THE NATURAL ENEMIES OF THE GODS! ...THE TROLLS!

16.

17

18

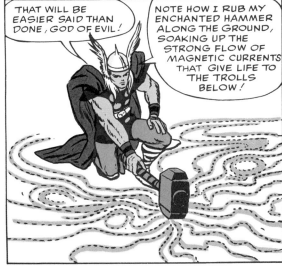

MEANWHILE, BACK ON EARTH, THE INCREDIBLE *HULK* EXECUTES ANOTHER OF HIS AWESOME LEAPS IN HIS EFFORT TO ESCAPE FROM *IRON MAN!*

CAPTAIN! DO *YOU* SEE WHAT *I* SEE?

IT'S THE *HULK,* MAKING ONE OF HIS PRODIGIOUS *LEAPS!*

SECONDS LATER, AN URGENT RADIO MESSAGE IS HEARD ABOARD THE SAME JETLINER...

ATTENTION, FLIGHT 738! THIS IS *IRON MAN!* HAVE YOU SEEN THE *HULK?* REPEAT — *HAVE YOU SEEN THE HULK?!*

SUFFERIN' CATS!!

HE..HE JUST WHIZZED PAST US! LOOKED LIKE HE WAS HEADIN' TOWARD DETROIT!

MUCH OBLIGED, CAPTAIN!

EVEN THOUGH I *SEE* IT...I DON'T BELIEVE IT!

FINALLY, ON THE GROUND AGAIN, INSIDE A HUGE AUTO FACTORY...

IRON MAN'S STILL AFTER ME! CAN'T LOSE HIM!

ATTENTION! CLEAR OUT, *ALL* OF YOU! THE HULK MUST BE STOPPED! TAKE COVER!

IT'S *IRON MAN!* BOY! HE DOESN'T HAVETA TELL ME *TWICE!*

YOU'RE WASTIN' YOUR TIME, *IRON MAN!* THESE PUNY THINGS CAN'T HURT THE *HULK!*

BUT NOW I'M SICK OF RUNNING! NOW IT'S *MY* TURN TO ATTACK!

HELP! SOMEBODY STOP 'IM! HE'S GONNA TEAR THIS PLACE *APART!!*

19.

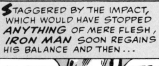

AND THEN, A TRAPDOOR SNAPS OPEN BENEATH THE UNPREPARED *LOKI!*

WHA...I'M *FALLING!*

ANT-MAN! YOU *DID* IT!

YES, *WASP!* IT ALL DEPENDED ON *LOKI* CARELESSLY STANDING IN THE RIGHT PLACE...AND HE *DID!*

THAT'S *IT*, MY LITTLE ALLIES! SEAL THE CHAMBER DOOR TIGHTLY! EVEN *LOKI* CAN'T ESCAPE FROM A *LEAD-LINED TANK!*

HE LANDED DOWN *HERE!* THIS IS WHERE THE TRUCKS THAT CARRY RADIOACTIVE WASTES FROM ATOMIC TESTS DUMP THEIR LOADS FOR EVENTUAL DISPOSAL IN THE OCEAN!

REST EASY, *THOR!* MY ANTS HAVE LOCKED *LOKI* INSIDE THIS IMPREGNABLE TANK WITH THE REST OF THE JUNK!

LOKI CANNOT REMAIN RADIOACTIVE FOR MORE THAN ANOTHER FEW MINUTES, AFTER WHICH I SHALL OPEN THE TANK AND RETURN HIM TO WHERE HE BELONGS!

WAIT! BEFORE WE SEPARATE, THE *WASP* AND I HAVE SOMETHING TO SAY!

EACH OF US HAS A DIFFERENT POWER! IF WE COMBINED FORCES, WE COULD BE ALMOST UNBEATABLE!

WORK AS A *TEAM?* WHY NOT? *I'M* FOR IT!

THERE IS MUCH *GOOD* WE MIGHT DO!

I'M SICK OF BEIN' HUNTED AND HOUNDED! I'D RATHER BE *WITH* YOU THAN *AGAINST* YOU! SO, WHETHER YOU LIKE IT OR NOT, *I'M* JOININ' THE ...THE...*HEY!* WHAT ARE YOU *CALLIN'* YOURSELVES?

THAT'S *RIGHT!* WE NEED A *NAME!*

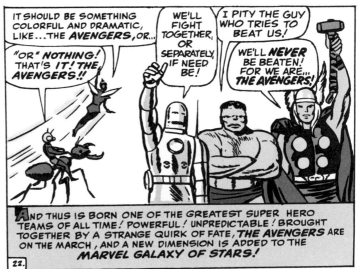

IT SHOULD BE SOMETHING COLORFUL AND DRAMATIC, LIKE...THE *AVENGERS,* OR...

"OR" *NOTHING!* THAT'S *IT!* THE *AVENGERS!!*

WE'LL FIGHT TOGETHER, OR SEPARATELY, IF NEED BE!

I PITY THE GUY WHO TRIES TO BEAT US!

WE'LL *NEVER* BE BEATEN! FOR WE ARE... *THE AVENGERS!*

AND THUS IS BORN ONE OF THE GREATEST SUPER HERO TEAMS OF ALL TIME! POWERFUL! UNPREDICTABLE! BROUGHT TOGETHER BY A STRANGE QUIRK OF FATE, *THE AVENGERS* ARE ON THE MARCH, AND A NEW DIMENSION IS ADDED TO THE *MARVEL GALAXY OF STARS!*

22.

26

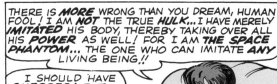

33

NOW, IN THE POWERFUL IDENTITY OF THE HULK AGAIN, I SHALL RETURN TO THE AVENGERS AND FINISH MY TASK! *THIS* TIME I WILL FIND A WAY TO MAKE THEM *DESTROY* THEMSELVES... AND EARTH SHALL THEN BE *MINE* FOR THE TAKING!

AS FOR THE *BOY*, HE IS OF NO FURTHER CONCERN! THERE IS NOTHING *HE* CAN DO TO STOP ME!

HE'S LEAVING! WHAT DO I DO *NOW?* WHAT *CAN* I DO?

A SHORT DISTANCE AWAY, A MULTIPLE ANTI-MISSILE MISSILE GUN, INVENTED BY ANTHONY STARK, IS ABOUT TO UNDERGO ITS FINAL TEST...

I TELL YOU, BILL, THAT TONY STARK IS A *GENIUS!* HE DREAMS UP THESE WEAPONS ALMOST FASTER THAN WE CAN *TEST* 'EM!

YEAH! HARD TO FIGURE WHERE HE GETS TIME TO BE A *PLAYBOY* AS WELL!

HE OUGHT TO *BE* HERE ANY MINUTE! CAN'T START THE TEST *WITHOUT* HIM!

MAYBE HE'LL SEND *IRON MAN* INSTEAD! BOY, IMAGINE HAVING A GUY LIKE *IRON MAN* ON YOUR PAYROLL!!

ON MY WAY TO *THE AVENGERS*, I MIGHT AS WELL DESTROY THIS WEAPON! IT WILL BE SOMETHING *ELSE* THE UNCOMPREHENDING *HULK* WILL BE BLAMED FOR!

IT'S THE *HULK!* HE'S STEALING OUR MISSILE GUN!

I MUST HAVE ACCIDENTALLY *TRIGGERED* THE DEVICE! *GOOD!* ANY DAMAGE I CAN DO TO THE HUMANS' WEAPONS WILL ULTIMATELY BENEFIT *ME!*

10

35

BUT, A BATTLE CAN BE WON BY *MORE* THAN STRENGTH! SEIZING THE HULK'S PONDEROUS HAND IN HIS OWN MIGHTY GRIP, *IRON MAN* SENDS A LOW VOLTAGE *ELECTRICAL CHARGE* OUT THRU HIS AMAZING, TRANSISTOR-POWERED FINGERS!

AND, WHILE THE *REAL* HULK WOULD HAVE ENDURED THE PAIN AND FOUGHT BACK IN A PAROXYSM OF SAVAGE FURY, THE SPACE PHANTOM POSSESSES NEITHER HIS COURAGE NOR HIS ALMOST LIMITLESS ENDURANCE, AND SO...

HE'S TOO STRONG! I'VE GOT TO ESCAPE!!

I DON'T UNDERSTAND! THAT ELECTRIC CHARGE WASN'T POWERFUL ENOUGH TO CAUSE THE HULK TO FLEE IN PANIC THAT WAY!! AND YET...

I'LL IMITATE THE SHAPE OF THAT SMALL FLYING INSECT!

AND SO, AS THE SPACE PHANTOM INSTANTANEOUSLY TRANSFORMS HIMSELF INTO A TINY WASP, THE *REAL* HULK REAPPEARS-- FROM LIMBO!

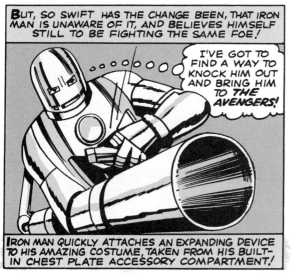

BUT, SO SWIFT HAS THE CHANGE BEEN, THAT IRON MAN IS UNAWARE OF IT, AND BELIEVES HIMSELF STILL TO BE FIGHTING THE SAME FOE!

I'VE GOT TO FIND A WAY TO KNOCK HIM OUT AND BRING HIM TO *THE AVENGERS!*

IRON MAN QUICKLY ATTACHES AN EXPANDING DEVICE TO HIS AMAZING COSTUME, TAKEN FROM HIS BUILT-IN CHEST PLATE ACCESSORY COMPARTMENT!

AND *THIS* SHOULD BE JUST THE THING TO DO THE TRICK... WITH APOLOGIES TO *THOR!* STRANGE, THOUGH... *THIS* TIME THE HULK DOESN'T LOOK FEARFUL!

CLICK

12

AND THE WASP'S INSTINCTS, HALF FEMALE INTUITION, HALF INSECT SUPER-SENSE, PROVE TO BE **RIGHT!** FOR MINUTES LATER...

GIANT-MAN'S PARTNER! WHAT A STROKE OF LUCK FOR ME!

A **WASP**-- ATTACKING ME!! BUT THAT'S **IMPOSSIBLE!** UNLESS-- IT'S NOT A **GENUINE** WASP!

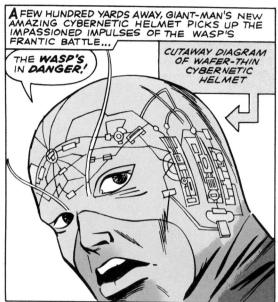

A FEW HUNDRED YARDS AWAY, GIANT-MAN'S NEW AMAZING CYBERNETIC HELMET PICKS UP THE IMPASSIONED IMPULSES OF THE WASP'S FRANTIC BATTLE...

THE **WASP'S** IN **DANGER!**

CUTAWAY DIAGRAM OF WAFER-THIN CYBERNETIC HELMET

THE CYBERNETIC IMPULSES COME FROM THE DIRECTION OF ANTHONY STARK'S FACTORY, JUST ACROSS GRAND CENTRAL PARKWAY!! **FOLLOW ME!**

HE DOESN'T SUSPECT THAT **I** AM REALLY ANTHONY STARK! ONCE INSIDE THE FACTORY, I'LL BE FIGHTING ON MY **HOME** GROUNDS!

HERE WE **ARE!** BUT EVERYTHING SEEMS NORMAL!

THROUGH THIS DOOR! THE IMPULSES ARE GETTING **STRONGER!**

WHY BOTHER WITH **DOORS?** I'D RATHER TEAR THE **WALLS** APART!

GUIDED TO THE WASP BY HIS SENSITIVE HELMET, THE **GIANT-MAN** DOESN'T NOTICE AN ASTONISHING CHANGE TAKING PLACE BEHIND HIM...

I NO LONGER NEED MY WASP-SHAPE! I SEE A FAR **BETTER** ONE TO "BORROW"!

JAN! THANK HEAVEN YOU'RE **SAFE!**

DON'T WORRY ABOUT **ME!** LOOK **BEHIND** YOU... **QUICK!**

15

BUT, BEFORE THE TWELVE-FOOT HIGH ADVENTURER CAN TURN AROUND, THE SPACE PHANTOM HAS TAKEN HIS IDENTITY, CAUSING THE REAL GIANT-MAN TO BE SENT INSTANTANEOUSLY TO LIMBO!

FAREWELL, GIANT-MAN! NOW I, THE SPACE PHANTOM, SHALL CONTINUE WHERE I LEFT OFF!

I'M WHIRLING INTO ANOTHER DIMENSION... A SHADOWY, SILENT WORLD!

THANK YOU, FEMALE HUMAN, FOR ACTING AS A *DECOY* FOR ME!

I--I *SAW* WHAT HAPPENED! YOU'RE *NOT* GIANT-MAN! YOU'VE TAKEN HIS FORM SOMEHOW... BUT *YOU'RE NOT HIM!*

I SAW IT, TOO! I DON'T KNOW HOW YOU TOOK OVER GIANT-MAN'S BODY... BUT THAT MUST BE WHAT HAPPENED *TO ME,* TOO!

SO! MY SECRET IS OUT! WELL, NO MATTER! I REALIZE NOW THAT I HAVE *NO NEED* FOR SECRECY!

BEGONE, WASP! I HAVE MORE IMPORTANT VICTIMS TO SLAY!

ONCE I HAVE DESTROYED THE AVENGERS, ALL OF EARTH WILL TREMBLE BEFORE THE POWER OF *THE SPACE PHANTOM!*

YEAH?

WELL, YOU FORGOT *ONE THING!* YOU TOOK THE *BIGGEST* BODY YOU COULD FIND, BUT NOT THE *STRONGEST!* THE HULK IS MORE POWERFUL THAN A *DOZEN* GIANT-MEN!

FOR THIS INDIGNITY, I WILL SLAY YOU *SLOWLY!*

I'VE GOT TO GET *HELP!* IF--IF ONLY I CAN FIND *THOR!*

16

41

BUT, IN ONE SPLIT SECOND, IRON MAN PRESSES A STUD ON HIS CHEST CONTROL PANEL, CAUSING HIS IRON SUIT TO BECOME RIGID, AND MAGNETIZING HIS IRON BOOTS SOLIDLY TO THE FLOOR!

THUMP!

SO! IT SEEMS THAT EACH OF YOU AVENGERS IS MORE POWERFUL THAN I HAD EXPECTED! BUT, NO MATTER! EVEN YOUR COMBINED MIGHT IS NOT GREAT ENOUGH TO SAVE YOU FROM THE SPACE PHANTOM!

BUT, THE OTHERS APPROACH!

I MUST ACT QUICKLY! I SHALL NOW TAKE IRON MAN'S FORM! NEITHER THE HULK NOR GIANT-MAN WILL SUSPECT...TILL IT IS TOO LATE!

AS THE SPACE PHANTOM SUDDENLY ASSUMES THE IDENTITY OF IRON-MAN, THE REAL GIANT-MAN DRAMATICALLY REAPPEARS, AND...

I'M BACK FROM LIMBO!! BUT... HOW CAN WE EVER DEFEAT THE QUICK-CHANGING SPACE PHANTOM??

COME ON, GIANT-MAN! DON'T JUST STAND THERE! HE TURNED HIMSELF INTO IRON MAN! I SAW HIM! GRAB HIM, BEFORE HE CAN CHANGE AGAIN!

18

42

AND, AS THE BATTLE CONTINUES IN STARK'S LONG ISLAND FACTORY, THE WASP DESPERATELY SEEKS HELP FROM THE ONE REMAINING MEMBER OF THE AVENGERS...

WE WERE TOLD TO CALL DR. DON BLAKE WHEN WE WANTED *THOR!* HE KNOWS HOW TO CONTACT HIM! I'M IN LUCK... THERE'S BLAKE *NOW!*

THE WASP!!

TROUBLE AT STARK FACTORY- NEED *THOR*

WAIT OUTSIDE IN THE RECEPTION ROOM WHILE I SEND FOR THOR!

WILL DO, DOC!

HMM...HE'D BE REAL *DREAMY* IF HE WAS A LITTLE *HUSKIER!*

SATISFIED THAT HE IS SAFE FROM PRYING EYES, THE LAME, MILD-LOOKING DOCTOR STAMPS HIS WALKING STICK ONCE UPON THE FLOOR, AND THEN...

...**A** STRONG, COMMANDING VOICE RINGS OUT INTO THE NEXT ROOM, AS THE WASP RETURNS...

WHO SUMMONS THE GOD OF THUNDER ?

I-- THE WASP!

THEN, AFTER QUICKLY TELLING HER STORY...

HE SOUNDS LIKE A BURLESQUE OF A COMIC HERO IN "MAD" MAGAZINE! BUT WITH THOSE SHOULDERS...THOSE EYES--WHO CARES *HOW* CORNY HE TALKS!!!

ON TO THE FACTORY OF TONY STARK! DEATH TO THE SPACE PHANTOM!

19

43

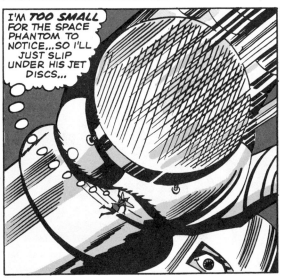

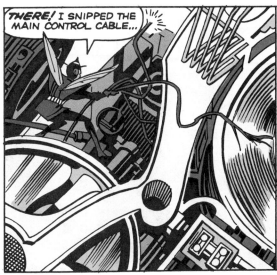

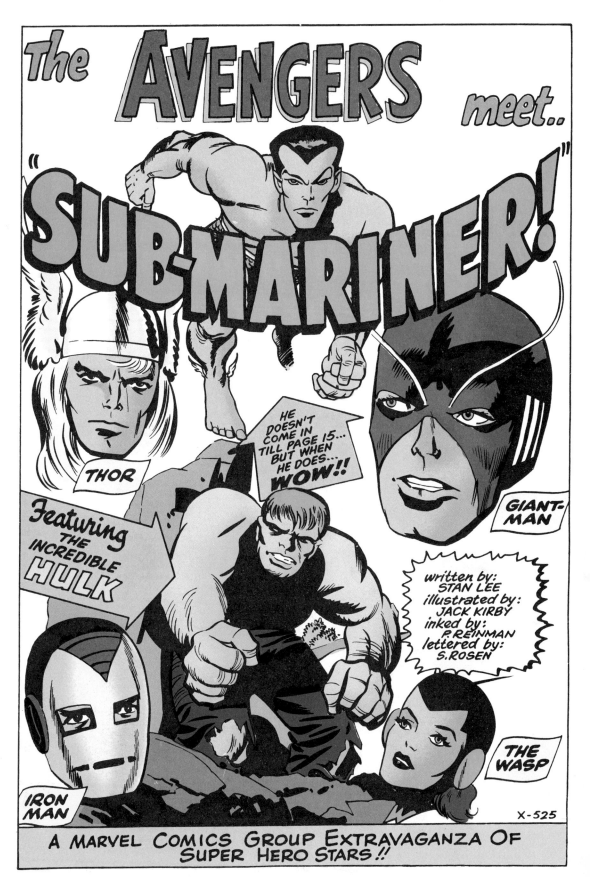

HOLDING THEIR MONTHLY MEETING IN THE HOME OF *TONY STARK*, MILLIONAIRE WEAPONS MAKER, THE *AVENGERS* DON'T SUSPECT HE IS REALLY ONE OF THEIR MEMBERS...THE ONE CALLED *IRON MAN!*

I TELL YOU WE'VE *GOT* TO FIND THE *HULK!* SO LONG AS HE IS RUNNING WILD, THERE'S NO TELLING *WHAT* HE'LL DO!*

IRON MAN IS *RIGHT!* SO SAYS *THOR!*

BUT HOW DO WE *FIND* HIM??

HE'S *ONE* JOKER YOU CAN'T FIND IN THE CLASSIFIED ADS!

*IN OUR LAST ISSUE, THE *HULK* UNEXPECT- EDLY QUIT THE AVENGERS!

ANTHONY STARK, WHOSE HOME WE'RE USING FOR THIS MEETING, IS NOT ONLY A FAMOUS *WEAPONS* INVENTOR, BUT A MASTER OF *ALL* KINDS OF TRANSISTOR-POWERED DEVICES!

...SUCH AS THIS *IMAGE PRO- JECTOR*, FOR EXAMPLE! IT WILL ENABLE ME TO PUT A SEARCH FOR THE HULK IN MOTION IN JUST A FEW SECONDS! WATCH...

AS IRON MAN ACTIVATES THE PROJECTOR, THE DEVICE WORKS LIKE AN ULTRA-FREQUENCY T.V. SET, BEAM- ING HIS IMAGE IN WHICHEVER DIRECTION HE HAS SET THE CIRCUITS FOR!

THOUGH I REMAIN HERE, MY *IMAGE* CAN BE SENT TO ANY DESTINATION... LIKE THIS!

TRAVELING AT THE SPEED OF LIGHT, IRON MAN'S ELECTRONIC IMAGE REACHES ITS FIRST OBJECTIVE... THE WORLD-FAMOUS SKYSCRAPER TOWER OF NEW YORK'S BAXTER BUILDING!

PERHAPS THE MOST MIRACULOUS PART OF STARK'S INVENTION IS THE FACT THAT THE IMAGE THAT IS PROJECTED CAN SEE, HEAR AND BE HEARD ALSO, WHEREVER IT IS...

FORGIVE MY SUDDEN APPEARANCE, FELLA! I HAVE A REQUEST TO MAKE!

SEND US A *LETTER*, PAL! I'VE GOT A *DATE* TONIGHT, AND I AIN'T BREAKIN' IT FOR ANY- ONE!

2.

* SEE *TALES OF SUSPENSE* #49 "*IRON MAN* AND *THE ANGEL*"

FINALLY, IRON MAN'S ELECTRONIC IMAGE RETURNS TO THE AVENGERS' MEETING ROOM...

I'M AFRAID I WASN'T TOO SUCCESSFUL! I ALERTED THE FANTASTIC FOUR, SPIDER-MAN AND THE X-MEN! BUT THEY'RE ALL PRETTY MUCH WRAPPED UP IN THEIR OWN AFFAIRS RIGHT NOW!

ANYWAY, I HAD A CHANCE TO TEST MY IMAGE PROJECTOR!

BEFORE WE SET OUT ON A TIME-CONSUMING WORLD-WIDE SEARCH, WHY DON'T WE CONTACT YOUNG RICK JONES!?

THOR'S RIGHT! HE'S THE ONLY ONE WHO CAN CONTROL THE HULK! PERHAPS HE CAN FIND HIM!

HE'S A SHORT-WAVE RADIO HAM! HE'S PROBABLY AT HIS SET RIGHT NOW!

AND, HALFWAY ACROSS THE COUNTRY, IN THE GREAT SOUTH-WEST, A GRIM-FACED TEEN-AGER RECEIVES THE AVENGERS' MESSAGE...

I UNDERSTAND, SIR! HE MIGHT BE IN THIS AREA ...IT'S HIS OLD STOMPING GROUNDS! I'LL START SEARCH-ING AT ONCE!

A HALF-HOUR LATER...

THE HULK IS TOO DANGEROUS TO ROAM OUT OF CONTROL! HE MIGHT... HEY! WHAT'S THAT?

STAY BACK, BOY! STAY BACK! DON'T COME ANY FURTHER!

THERE'S SOME KINDA MONSTER LOOSE BACK THERE! BIGGEST CREATURE I EVER SAW! I'M GOIN' TO NOTIFY THE POLICE RIGHT NOW!

I'M IN LUCK! IT MUST BE THE HULK! I'VE GOT TO REACH HIM BEFORE THE POLICE DO!

I WAS RIGHT! THERE HE IS NOW!

BUT WHAT'S HE DOING? WHY'S HE REACHING INTO THAT LAKE ??

HERE IT IS! I KNEW I'D FIND IT!

SOME FOOL STRANGER DROVE THIS THING RIGHT INTO THE LAKE AND RAN OFF AS SOON AS HE SAW ME!

HULK! ...IT'S ME! RICK! LISTEN TO ME...

5.

52

THE *POLICE* WILL BE COMING AFTER YOU SOON! YOU'VE GOT TO RETURN TO YOUR CAVE.!

BAH! WHY SHOULD I *RUN?* I'VE DONE NOTHING WRONG!

BUT PEOPLE ARE *SCARED* OF YOU... YOU *KNOW* THAT! AND IN THEIR PANIC THEY TRY TO *DESTROY* WHAT THEY FEAR!

SWAYED BY RICK'S WORDS, THE HULK HURLS HIMSELF INTO THE AIR WITH THE MIGHTIEST LEG MUSCLES ON EARTH, AS THE SLIM TEEN-AGER CLINGS TO HIS SHOULDERS!

A SHORT TIME LATER, THEY ENTER A HIDDEN CAVE THAT LEADS DEEP UNDER THE GROUND...

I'M *SICK* OF RUNNING! WHY SHOULD *I* FEAR OTHER HUMANS? I CAN SMASH THEM *ALL!*

Y-YOU DON'T *MEAN* THAT, HULK! YOU'RE TIRED! YOU NEED A REST!

SOON, THE INCREDIBLE CREATURE STANDS IN FRONT OF A STRANGE RAY MACHINE... A MACHINE BUILT BY THE MAN HE ONCE WAS..

DON'T MOVE NOW! I'LL FLIP THE SWITCH!

SECONDS LATER, THE MASSIVE HERCULEAN BODY IS BOMBARDED BY A BLAST OF BLINDING GAMMA RAYS...

GAMMA RAYS! THE MYSTERIOUS DISCOVERY OF BRUCE BANNER, SO MANY MONTHS AGO! THE RAYS THAT TURNED BANNER HIMSELF INTO... *THE HULK!*

FINALLY, THE ONSLAUGHT ENDS! AND, WHERE STOOD THE TITANIC FORM OF THE HULK, WE NOW FIND THE STUNNED, EXHAUSTED FIGURE OF *DR. BRUCE BANNER,* ATOMIC SCIENTIST.

THE NIGHTMARE IS OVER! I'M MY-SELF AGAIN!

IT'S LUCKY FOR US! YOU GET *WORSE* EACH TIME YOU BECOME THE HULK! YOU GET HARDER TO CON-TROL!

YOU GOTTA *REST* NOW, DOC! EVERY-THING'S GONNA BE OKAY!

LOCK THE CAVERN DOOR, RICK! AND DON'T LEAVE ME... IN CASE I CHANGE AGAIN! I DON'T *DARE!*

AND, SO THE BOY'S LONG VIGIL BEGINS...

IT'S ALL *MY* FAULT! HE BECAME THE *HULK* WHEN HE SAVED MY LIFE BY LETTIN' THE GAMMA RAYS HIT *HIM!* I...I CAN'T EVER DESERT HIM...

6.

BUT BEHIND THE MASSIVE DOOR, AS THE NIGHT DRAGS ON...

CAN'T SLEEP! CAN'T STOP THINKING OF...THE HULK! IT'S THE GAMMA RAYS...

RICK DIDN'T GIVE ME A STRONG ENOUGH DOSE...CAN'T REMAIN AS BRUCE BANNER...

BUT...WHY SHOULD I REMAIN AS THE WEAK BANNER??

WHY SHOULDN'T I BE THE HULK?? WHY BE A PUNY SCIENTIST WHEN I CAN BE THE MOST POWERFUL MAN WALKING THE EARTH??!

AND THEN, WITH THE SUDDEN FURY OF A THUNDERCLAP...

HE'S THE HULK AGAIN! AND HE'S STRONGER THAN EVER!

HULK!! WAIT! STOP!!

NO USE! HE DOESN'T EVEN HEAR ME! HE'S COMPLETELY OUT OF CONTROL!

FRANTIC MINUTES LATER, AT A LOCAL TEEN BRIGADE RADIO ROOM...

LET ME AT THAT SET! CONDITION RED!

LOOK GUYS! IT'S RICK!

GRIMLY, THE YOUNG LEADER OF THE TEEN BRIGADE SENDS OUT AN URGENT CALL...

CALLING AVENGERS! CALLING AVENGERS! HAVE LOCATED HULK!

HE'S IN NEW MEXICO! SECTOR B! ON THE RAMPAGE! COME AT ONCE!

AND, TWO THOUSAND MILES TO THE EAST...AT THE HOME OF TONY STARK...

COME AT ONCE!

THIS IS IT! THE HULK MUST BE STOPPED!!

7.

EVEN THE OTHER AVENGERS DON'T KNOW THAT TONY STARK IS REALLY *IRON MAN!*

...JUST AS *I* DON'T KNOW *THEIR* SECRET IDENTITIES! WELL, I'VE GOT TO ALERT THEM NOW!

LATER, AT THE LAB OF *GIANT-MAN* AND THE *WASP*, A PRIVATE PHONE RINGS, AND...

IT'S IRON MAN! THE HULK HAS BEEN FOUND!

WE'LL LEAVE AT ONCE! GET THE LOCATION FROM HIM!

I CAN TRAVEL FASTER ON MY FLYING ANT... SO TAKE YOUR *SHRINKING* CAPSULE!

DIDN'T ANYONE EVER TEACH YOU TO SAY "PLEASE," LOVER BOY?

NOW FOR THE HULK! GIANT-MAN AND THE WASP ARE ON THE WAY!

AND I CALLED *THOR'S* PRIVATE NUMBER AND LEFT A MESSAGE...

WE'LL REACH THE AIRPORT IN MINUTES AND HITCH A RIDE ON THE FASTEST JET!

KNOW SOMETHING, HANDSOME? YOU LOOK LIKE THE POOR MAN'S *BEN HUR* ON THAT SILLY ANT!

WHILE AT THE CONSULTING ROOM OF DR. DON BLAKE ...

IT'S BEEN A BUSY DAY AND I'M RATHER TIRED, JANE! SO I'M CLOSING THE OFFICE EARLY!

OH, DON, IF ONLY YOU DIDN'T *PAMPER* YOURSELF SO! IF ONLY YOU WERE MORE *RUGGED!*

BUT, ONCE ALONE IN HIS OFFICE, THE "PAMPERED" DR. BLAKE STRIKES HIS WALKING STICK ONCE UPON THE FLOOR ...

...AND THE MIGHTY *THOR* APPEARS!!

NOW FOR THE HULK!!

IRON MAN'S MESSAGE SAID HE WAS SIGHTED IN NEW MEXICO, SECTOR B!

IT WILL NOT TAKE THE *AVENGERS* LONG TO REACH THE SPOT, FOR WE EACH HAVE OUR OWN UNIQUE METHODS OF TRAVEL!

8.

SOME TIME LATER, HAVING BEEN FIRST TO LEAVE, *IRON MAN* IS FIRST TO ARRIVE AT THE APPOINTED PLACE, ONLY TO SEE...

THERE'S RICK! BUT WHY IS HE TRYING TO WAVE ME *AWAY*??

THE AVENGER IN THE IRON GARB GETS HIS ANSWER ONE STAGGERING SECOND LATER...

WHAM!

RECOVERING FROM A BLOW THAT WOULD HAVE FINISHED ANY HUMAN NOT PROTECTED BY AN ARMORED SUIT, IRON MAN QUICKLY MANIPULATES HIS SHORT-RANGE POWER REPULSER, AND THEN...

ONE BRIEF TRANSISTOR-POWERED ENERGY BLAST SHOULD GIVE ME A FEW SECONDS TIME TO THINK OF A PLAN!

I'LL DIRECT THE BEAM AT THOSE BOULDERS IN FRONT OF THE HULK! THIS WON'T *STOP* HIM, BUT IT'S SURE TO SLOW HIM DOWN!

BAH! IS *THAT* THE BEST YOU CAN DO?

9

WHILE UP ABOVE, IRON MAN CON-TINUES TO TRY TO REASON WITH THE HULK...

WE DON'T WANT TO *FIGHT* YOU, HULK! BUT WE CAN'T LET YOU RUN AMOK THROUGH THE COUNTRYSIDE! YOU'VE GOT TO STAY WITH US... WORK WITH US AS A *TEAM*!

NO! YOU CAN'T FOOL ME! YOU ALL HATE ME...FEAR ME BECAUSE I'M THE *STRONG-EST!* IF I STAY WITH YOU, YOU'LL FIND SOME WAY TO *DESTROY* ME!

MEANTIME, DIRECTLY UNDER THE HULK'S FEET, THE PEBBLES HAVE DAMMED UP THE UNDERGROUND STREAM, AND THE RUSHING WATER, HAVING NO PLACE TO GO...

...BURSTS TO THE SURFACE, CAUSING THE GROUND UNDER-FOOT TO CRUMBLE...

THAT MUST BE THE WORK OF *ANT-MAN*, TO TRAP THE HULK!!

BUT THE PLAN PROVES TO BE IN VAIN, FOR THE HULK'S UNBELIEVABLY STRONG LEG MUSCLES CATAPULT HIM TO SAFETY...

DON'T *COUNT* ON IT, BUSTER! I'M NOT EXACTLY *HELPLESS* UP HERE!

HERE'S WHERE I SNAP THAT ARMOR PLATE OF YOURS LIKE A TIN CAN!!

DID I EVER TELL YOU ABOUT MY MAGNETIC REPULSERS?? HOW THEY CAN SPIN A BODY AROUND IN THE AIR, ATTRACTED BY ITS IRON CONTENT!??

LET *ME* HAVE HIM, IRON MAN!

DIZZY FROM THE RAPID WHIRLING HE HAS ENDURED, THE *HULK* SEIZES A NATURAL ROCK FORMATION BELOW AND USES IT TO BREAK HIS SPIN, AS *THOR* APPEARS ON THE SCENE...

THIS'LL SLOW ME DOWN!

HEAR ME, HULK! I AM NOT AS MERCIFUL AS IRON MAN! I ORDER YOU TO RETURN WITH THE AVENGERS, OR SUFFER MY WRATH!

JUST WAIT'LL MY HEAD CLEARS, LONG HAIR, AND THEN WE'LL *SEE* WHO DOES THE SUFFERIN'!

CAREFUL, THOR! HE'S CAPABLE OF *ANYTHING*!

11.

60

THROUGHOUT THE COUNTRYSIDE, THE SEARCH GOES ON...THE SEARCH FOR THE *HULK!!*

HAVE I SEEN THE *HULK??* ARE YOU *KIDDIN'?!!*

IF I EVER SAW *HIM*...I'D MAKE THIS TRUCK *FLY* OVER THE ROAD!

BUT LATER, WHEN THE DRIVER DUMPS HIS LOAD OF GRAVEL INTO A STREAM, HE IS UNAWARE THAT HE IS DUMPING *MORE* THAN PLAIN GRAVEL...

SO FAR, SO GOOD! THEY'LL *NEVER* FIND ME NOW!

DUE TO HIS INCREDIBLY POWERFUL LUNGS, THE HULK CAN REMAIN UNDERWATER FOR LONG PERIODS OF TIME, ALTHOUGH, LIKE A WHALE, HE *MUST* SURFACE FOR AIR EVENTUALLY...!

THE GULF STREAM ISN'T TOO FAR FROM HERE...

FINALLY, AFTER DAYS IN THE WATER, EVEN THE HULK'S MIGHTY BODY IS ON THE VERGE OF COMPLETE EXHAUSTION! AND THEN, AS HE FLOATS AIMLESSLY IN THE COLD ATLANTIC...

HARD TO STARBOARD! THERE'S SOMEONE *FLOATING* OUT THERE!

IT *CAN'T* BE HUMAN! AND YET...

LOOK! IT'S THE *HULK!* HE..HE'LL DROWN US *ALL!*

DON'T BE A *FOOL,* SAILOR! HE'S MORE DEAD THAN ALIVE! PUT HIM ON DECK AND NOTIFY WASHINGTON IMMEDIATELY!

OOF! PULL *HARDER!* HE MUST WEIGH A *TON!*

BUT NOW OUR SCENE SHIFTS TO A SECRET UNDERSEA CHAMBER WHERE WE FIND...

SO FAR EVERYTHING IS WORKING OUT *PERFECTLY!*

LITTLE DOES THE HULK REALIZE THAT HIS EVERY MOVEMENT IS BEING FOLLOWED BY THE MONARCH OF THE SEA, PRINCE NAMOR, THE *SUB-MARINER!!*

THE HULK'S STRENGTH WILL RETURN SOONER THAN THE HUMANS SUSPECT! AND WHEN IT DOES...AND WHEN HE ABANDONS THE SHIP... *I'LL* BE WAITING FOR HIM!!

15.

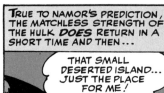

TRUE TO NAMOR'S PREDICTION, THE MATCHLESS STRENGTH OF THE HULK *DOES* RETURN IN A SHORT TIME AND THEN...

THAT SMALL DESERTED ISLAND... JUST THE PLACE FOR ME!

I CAN GRAB ME A PASSING SHIP ANYTIME I *WANT* TO!

BUT FIRST, I WANT A PLACE WHERE I CAN BE ALONE...WHERE I CAN PLAN MY NEXT MOVES AGAINST THE HUMAN RACE THAT HATES ME!

BUT WHEN THE MIGHTY CREATURE REACHES THE ISLE, HE FINDS...

I HAVE BEEN *WAITING* FOR YOU, HULK! AND YOU SHOULD BE FLATTERED! FOR, NORMALLY, THE *SUB-MARINER* WAITS FOR NOBODY!

THE *SUB-MARINER*!!

GET *OFF* THIS ISLAND, FISH-MAN! I'M SICK OF LOOKIN' AT PUNY HUMANS! SICK OF THE SOUND OF THEIR VOICES!

BRAIN-LESS DOLT! YOU CALL *ME* HUMAN?! I AM *NAMOR*, PRINCE OF ATLANTIS!

I DON'T CARE *WHO* YOU ARE! YOU *LOOK* LIKE A HUMAN! AND THAT'S ENOUGH TO MAKE ME WANT TO TOSS YOU CLEAR BACK TO THE MAINLAND!

WHAT?? YOU DARE LAY A HAND ON MY ROYAL PERSONAGE??!

YOU HAVE MUCH TO LEARN, LANDBOUND CLOD! AND *THIS* IS YOUR FIRST LESSON!

YOU KNOW SOMETHIN', LITTLE MAN?? YOU SHOOT YOUR MOUTH OFF TOO MUCH!

THIS'LL QUIET YOU DOWN FOR A WHILE...LIKE *FOREVER!*

YOU *STILL* THINK YOU ARE DEALING WITH A HELPLESS *HUMAN*, DO YOU?? WELL, WE SHALL *SEE!*

16.

THE HUMANS ARE MY SWORN ENEMIES! BECAUSE OF THEM, I HAVE LOST MY BIRTH-RIGHT, MY PEOPLE, EVERYTHING I HOLD DEAR! *

I DON'T GO FOR ALL THAT FLOWERY TALK, BUT I HATE HUMANS, TOO!

*SEE FANTASTIC FOUR ANNUAL, #1 — EDITOR.

THEN IT IS AGREED! OUR FIRST MISSION SHALL BE TO DELIVER A SMASHING DEFEAT TO THE ACCURSED AVENGERS!

I SHALL SUMMON MY ELECTRONICALLY CONTROLLED COMMAND SHIP TO TAKE US TO OUR DESTINATION!

BUT ONCE INSIDE THE SHIP...

I'LL STRING ALONG FOR A WHILE, THEN SMASH HIM WHEN HE'S OFF-GUARD!

HE'S TOO STRONG! TOO UNDEPEND-ABLE! WHEN HE'S SERVED HIS PURPOSE, I'LL DESTROY HIM!!

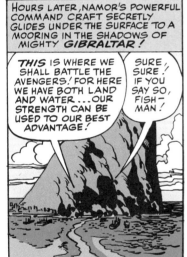

HOURS LATER, NAMOR'S POWERFUL COMMAND CRAFT SECRETLY GLIDES UNDER THE SURFACE TO A MOORING IN THE SHADOWS OF MIGHTY GIBRALTAR!

THIS IS WHERE WE SHALL BATTLE THE AVENGERS! FOR HERE WE HAVE BOTH LAND AND WATER... OUR STRENGTH CAN BE USED TO OUR BEST ADVANTAGE!

SURE, SURE! IF YOU SAY SO, FISH-MAN!

LATER, AT AVENGERS H.Q....

THERE'S NO DOUBT ABOUT IT! THE MESSAGE IS GENUINE! SUB-MARINER AND THE HULK HAVE JOINED FORCES... AND CHALLENGED US TO BATTLE!

THEN THIS TIME THERE CAN BE NO PULLING OF PUNCHES...NO MERCY ASKED OR GIVEN! YES, BY ASGARD!! THIS TIME WE FIGHT TO THE FINISH!

I HOPE IT WON'T BE YOUR FINISH, HANDSOME! BECAUSE I'M STILL WAITING TO SEE WHAT YOU'D LOOK LIKE IN AN IVY LEAGUE SUIT AND A CREW CUT! WITH THOSE SHOULDERS, THOSE EYES...MMMM...

AREN'T YOU EVER GONNA GROW UP, WASP? HAVEN'T YOU ANYTHING ELSE ON YOUR MIND??

WELL, HAPPY DAY! DO I FINALLY SEE A GLINT OF GREEN IN THOSE BIG BLUE EYES OF YOURS??

NOW PUT ME DOWN, YOU BIG SHOWOFF! THIS IS VERY UNDIGNIFIED!!

18.

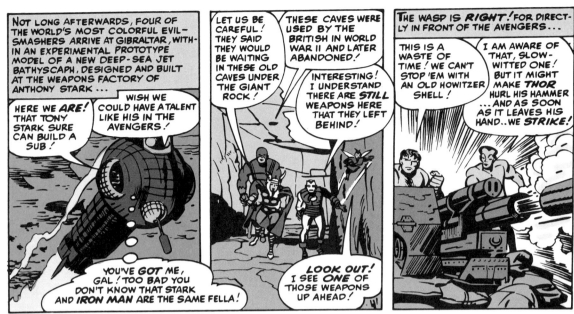

HE HIT ME WITH AN *EMERY DUST PELLET*! IT'LL MAKE MY METAL JOINTS STIFFEN! I NEVER EXPECTED...

GO TO HIS *AID*, MY GIANT ALLY! I SHALL KEEP OUR TWO FOES AT BAY WITH MY ENCHANTED MALLET!

NEVER SAW ANYTHING HAPPEN SO FAST! HE'S STIFF AS A BOARD... CAN'T MOVE!

WASP! FLY THROUGH THESE CAVES, *QUICKLY!!* SEE IF YOU CAN FIND ANY OLD, ABANDONED *OXYGEN* EQUIPMENT WHICH MAY STILL BE OPERATIONAL!

WILL DO, LOVER BOY!

FOR THE NEXT FEW SECONDS, AS THE WONDERFUL FLYING WASP FRANTICALLY SEARCHES THE WINDING CAVES, THOR'S THUNDERING HAMMER RICOCHETS FROM WALL TO WALL...

NEVER HAVE I WITNESSED SUCH AN AWESOME DISPLAY OF NAKED POWER!

AND EXACTLY 58 SECONDS LATER...

TO ME, MY WONDROUS MALLET!

GOOD WORK, WASP! JUST WHAT I WANTED!

THIS OLD AIR RAID LIFE-SAVING EQUIPMENT SHOULD DO THE TRICK!

THERE! IT'S PUMPING OUT THE EMERY DUST! HE'S STARTING TO MOVE!

MEANTIME ...

THEY'RE UP TO SOMETHING ELSE! I'VE GOT TO FOLLOW!

TOGETHER THEY'RE SO POWERFUL ...I-I'M *WORRIED*, FOR THE FIRST TIME!

THE AVENGERS ARE JUST ON THE OTHER SIDE OF THIS WALL! NOW STAY BACK, FISH-MAN! I'LL SHOW YOU WHAT THE HULK CAN DO!

I'LL HUMOR THE THICK-SKINNED FOOL FOR NOW...WHILE I STILL NEED AN ALLY!

20.

COVER YOUR EARS, LITTLE MAN! THEY'LL HEAR *THIS* HALFWAY TO CALCUTTA!

NOT HAVING TIME TO TAKE COVER, THE UNSEEN WASP BEARS THE FULL BRUNT OF THE HULK'S SAVAGE EARDRUM-SHATTERING BLOW, AS THE TINY ADVENTURESS SUDDENLY BLACKS OUT!

SECONDS LATER, STILL DAZED AND WEAK, SHE TRIES VALIANTLY TO DODGE THE STONES THAT FALL ALL AROUND HER!

TH-THEY MAY BE ONLY *PEBBLES*, BUT THEY'RE LIKE HUGE *BOULDERS* TO ME!

BUT, BEFORE THE HULK CAN LAUNCH ANOTHER BLOW IN HIS EFFORT TO BRING THE WALLS DOWN UPON THE AVENGERS, THE FIGHTING-MAD TRIO THUNDERS TOWARD THE SOURCE OF THE SOUND...

THEY DON'T *SEE* ME! I-I'LL BE *TRAMPLED!*

WHEW! THANK HEAVENS THE GROUND HERE IS SO UNEVEN!

I'VE HAD ENOUGH OF BEING A LONE WOLF! I'M NOT LEAVING *GIANT-MAN'S* SHOULDER AGAIN TILL WE'RE *OUT* OF HERE!

WHILE DIRECTLY *ABOVE* THE AVENGERS...

YOUR FISTS ARE TOO *SLOW*, MY BESTIAL PARTNER! I HAVE MODIFIED THIS OLD AIR RAID ALARM SO THAT ITS SHRILL, HIGH PIERCING BLAST WILL DESTROY ANY LIVING BEING WHO COMES TOO CLOSE!

21.

BUT, IN A LAST EFFORT, NAMOR USES HIS WINGED FEET TO WHIRL HIMSELF AROUND, AND...

THIS WILL PROVE THAT NONE CAN DEFEAT THE MONARCH OF THE SEA!

IRON MAN HAS REPAIRED HIS ARMOR! I'LL DRIVE NAMOR TOWARDS HIM WITH MY HAMMER!

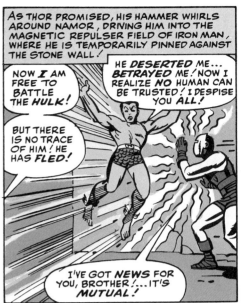

AS THOR PROMISED, HIS HAMMER WHIRLS AROUND NAMOR, DRIVING HIM INTO THE MAGNETIC REPULSER FIELD OF IRON MAN, WHERE HE IS TEMPORARILY PINNED AGAINST THE STONE WALL!

NOW I AM FREE TO BATTLE THE HULK!

BUT THERE IS NO TRACE OF HIM! HE HAS FLED!

HE DESERTED ME... BETRAYED ME! NOW I REALIZE NO HUMAN CAN BE TRUSTED! I DESPISE YOU ALL!

I'VE GOT NEWS FOR YOU, BROTHER!...IT'S MUTUAL!

YOU'RE GROWING WEAKER BY THE MINUTE, NAMOR! WHY DON'T YOU GIVE UP? LET'S TRY AND TALK THIS OUT!

NEVER! WHILE LIFE REMAINS WITHIN ME, I SHALL FIGHT YOU!! I SHALL FIGHT ALL MANKIND!

WITH ONE LAST PRODIGIOUS EFFORT, THE SUB-MARINER CRACKS THE WALL BEHIND HIM, AS THE WATER, TRICKLING DOWN FROM ABOVE, DRIPS UPON HIS STEEL-MUSCLED BODY...

WATER!!! AT LAST---WATER!

THEN, AS NEW STRENGTH, NEW POWER SURGES INTO EVERY FIBER OF HIS BEING...

I'M FREE! NOTHING CAN HOLD ME NOW!

THOR! HE'S ESCAPING! ONLY YOUR HAMMER CAN STOP HIM! HURL IT!

NO! I HAVE TOO MUCH RESPECT FOR HIS VALOR! NAMOR HAS EARNED HIS ESCAPE!

THOR'S RIGHT! IT'S A PITY THE SUB-MARINER ISN'T ON OUR SIDE!

WE'VE MADE A BAD MISTAKE! HE DOESN'T FIGHT BY OUR RULES! WE MAY LIVE TO REGRET THIS!

AND AS THE PRINCE OF THE SEA RETURNS TO HIS NATURAL HABITAT...

ON LAND, I COULD NOT DEFEAT THEM ALL! BUT I PRAY WE MEET AGAIN... UNDER THE SEA! AHH, HOW DIFFERENT THE ENDING THEN SHALL BE!

AND SO, THE AVENGERS RETURN HOME, WEARY AND SAD OF HEART! FOR THEY ALL SENSE THAT THE ADVENTURE THEY HAVE JUST CONCLUDED IS BUT THE PRELUDE TO A FAR BIGGER, A FAR MORE DANGEROUS ADVENTURE TO COME!!

ONE THING YOU HAVE LEARNED TO EXPECT FROM THE MIGHTY MARVEL GROUP IS...THE UNEXPECTED! AND WE PROMISE YOU THAT THE MOVIE-LENGTH TALE IN NEXT ISSUE'S AVENGERS WILL FEATURE SUPER-CHARACTERS AND SUPER-SURPRISES TO EXCEED YOUR WILDEST EXPECTATIONS! End

25.

REMEMBER THE AWESOME BATTLE BETWEEN THE HULK, SUB-MARINER AND THE AVENGERS LAST ISSUE? AFTER THE MIGHTY HULK VANISHED, SUB-MARINER FOUND THE ODDS TOO GREAT...

WE'RE TOO LATE! HE'S GETTING AWAY!

THINKING HIMSELF BETRAYED BY THE HULK, HIS HATRED OF THE HUMAN RACE GREATER THAN EVER BEFORE, THE VENGEFUL MONARCH OF THE SEA RETURNS TO THE DEEP...

THEY HAVE WON THE FIRST BATTLE, BUT THE FINAL VICTORY WILL YET BE MINE! FOR I SHALL NEVER REST UNTIL ALL OF MANKIND PAYS THE HOMAGE THAT IS RIGHTFULLY DUE TO *NAMOR*, PRINCE OF ATLANTIS!

DEEPER AND DEEPER SWIMS THE TRAGIC, ALMOST HUMAN RULER OF THE SEA! BUT NOWHERE IN THE VAST, ENDLESS DEPTHS OF THE OCEAN DOES HE FIND THE PEACE HE CRAVES!

AND NOWHERE DOES HE FIND HIS VANISHED RACE--THE PROUD, ONCE-MIGHTY HORDES OF ATLANTIS, WHO FLED FROM NAMOR WHEN THEY FELT HIS LOYALTY WAS DIVIDED BETWEEN THEM AND THE HUMANS!*

GONE--ALL GONE! WILL I EVER FIND MY PEOPLE AGAIN??

* FOR A MORE DETAILED ACCOUNT, REFER TO *FANTASTIC FOUR* ANNUAL #1... "SUB-MARINER VERSUS THE HUMAN RACE!" —EDITOR

TO THE TIRELESS PRINCE NAMOR, TIME AND DISTANCE ARE ALMOST MEANINGLESS, AND SO IT IS THAT WE FIND HIM, HOURS LATER, STANDING ATOP AN ICE FLOE IN THE NORTH SEA, STILL WRAPPED UP IN HIS OWN BITTER THOUGHTS...

I'LL *NEVER* STOP SEARCHING! I'LL NEVER FORFEIT MY BIRTH-RIGHT WHILE A BREATH OF LIFE REMAINS!

BUT FINALLY, HIS DARK MUSINGS ARE INTERRUPTED, AS HE SEES...

ON THE ICE AHEAD-- A HUMAN VILLAGE! I SEE MASSES OF ACCURSED *HUMANS!*

AND THE KEEN-EYED NAMOR IS RIGHT! A FEW HUNDRED YARDS AWAY, AN ISOLATED TRIBE OF ESKIMOS BOWS DOWN IN A STRANGE RITUAL...

OH, MIGHTY LORD OF THE FROZEN ICE, HEAR OUR PRAYERS...

2

UNTIL, FINALLY--NAUGHT REMAINS BUT A FROZEN, PETRIFIED FIGURE IN A STATE OF SUSPENDED ANIMATION... A FIGURE WHICH DRIFTS PAST THE UNDERSEA CRAFT OF-- *THE AVENGERS!*

STOP THE ENGINES, IRON MAN! THERE IS SOMEONE *OUT* THERE!

LOOKS LIKE A *HUMAN!* BUT HOW IS IT *POSSIBLE??*

CAUTIOUSLY OPENING THE AIR-TIGHT ESCAPE HATCH, THE HUGE HAND OF GIANT-MAN SEIZES THE RIGID FIGURE, AND...

I'VE GOT HIM!

WHO CAN HE *BE?* WHY IS HE FROZEN SOLID?

LOOK! BENEATH HIS TATTERED CLOTHES-- SOME SORT OF COLORFUL *COSTUME!*

WAIT! DON'T YOU *RECOGNIZE* IT?? IT'S THE FAMOUS RED, WHITE AND BLUE GARB OF-- *CAPTAIN AMERICA!*

THE WASP IS *RIGHT!*

CAN THIS REALLY BE THE FAMOUS SHIELD OF THE ONCE-MIGHTY CRIME-FIGHTER?

AND HIS FACE MASK -- WITH THE PROUD LETTER "A" ON IT! IT *MUST* BE HIM!

ALL OF YOU-- *LISTEN!* HE ISN'T DEAD! HE'S *BREATHING!* HIS EYES-- THEY'RE *FLICKERING!*

4

SUDDENLY, WITH AN EAR-SPLITTING CRY, THE POWERFUL FIGURE SPRINGS UPWARD --WITH AGONIZING SHOCK REFLECTED IN HIS EYES!

BUCKY-- BUCKY! LOOK OUT!

YOU CAN'T KILL HIM! YOU CAN'T KILL BUCKY! I WON'T LET YOU! I'LL SMASH YOU ALL!

THOR! IRON MAN! STOP HIM! HE'S GONE MAD!

BUT, AS SUDDENLY AS IT STARTED, THE LEGENDARY HERO'S WRATH SUBSIDES, AND THEN...

IT'S USELESS! I REMEMBER NOW! HE IS DEAD--HE IS,! AND NOTHING ON EARTH CAN CHANGE THAT!

AND THEN, AS REALIZATION DAWNS, THE HANDSOME HEAD SLOWLY TURNS... THE CLEAR BLUE EYES TAKE IN THE AWESOME FIGURES SUR-ROUNDING HIM...

WHERE AM I? HOW DID I GET HERE? WHO ARE YOU??

THAT'S WHAT WE WERE ABOUT TO ASK YOU!

WHO AM I??

FOR A MOMENT, I HAD ALMOST FORGOTTEN MYSELF!

BUT I AM NOT LUCKY ENOUGH TO FORGET FOREVER!

--TO FORGET THAT I WAS ONCE THE MAN THE WORLD CALLED--CAPTAIN AMERICA!

5

78

SLOWLY, ALMOST HALTINGLY, THE INCREDIBLE TALE BEGINS TO ISSUE FORTH FROM THE LIPS OF THE MIGHTY MAN WITH THE TRAGEDY-HAUNTED EYES...

IT SEEMS LIKE ONLY YESTERDAY--BUT IT WAS MORE THAN TWENTY YEARS AGO THAT MY TEEN-AGE PAL, BUCKY--AND I--WHILE ACTING AS SECURITY GUARDS AT AN E.T.O.* ARMY BASE-- TRIED TO STOP AN EXPLOSIVE-FILLED DRONE PLANE FROM TAKING TO THE AIR!

WE'RE TOO LATE, BUCKY! WE'LL HAVE TO GO AFTER IT IN ANOTHER PLANE!

NO! DON'T STOP! I THINK I CAN REACH IT, CAP!

HAH! THUS DO I TRIUMPH OVER CAPTAIN AMERICA AND BUCKY! IF THEY REACH THE PLANE, THEY DIE! AND IF THEY FAIL, AMERICA LOSES ONE OF ITS NEWEST WEAPONS!

*E.T.O.: EUROPEAN THEATER OF OPERATIONS.

THE BOY WAS CLOSER-- HE REACHED THE PLANE! BUT CAPTAIN AMERICA HIMSELF CANNOT HOLD ON!

CAN'T MAKE IT! DROP OFF INTO THE WATER, LAD! DON'T TRY TO GO IT ALONE!

NO! I CAN BRING THE PLANE BACK --I KNOW I CAN!

BUCKY! LET GO! IT MIGHT BE BOOBY-TRAPPED! YOU CAN'T DEACTIVATE THE BOMB WITHOUT ME! DROP OFF!

YOU'RE RIGHT, CAP! I SEE THE FUSE! IT'S GONNA BLOW!

"AND THOSE WERE THE LAST WORDS THAT BRAVE, WONDERFUL LAD EVER UTTERED...MAY THE LORD REST HIS SOUL!

BUCKY!! IT EXPLODED! BUCKY'S GONE!

"AS FOR ME, I DIDN'T CARE IF I LIVED OR DIED! I STRUCK THE WATER OFF THE COAST OF NEWFOUNDLAND AND PLUMMETTED LIKE A ROCK--WITH BUCKY'S FACE ETCHED BEFORE ME! AND THAT IS THE LAST THING I REMEMBER!"

HE'S GONE---AND I--- WITH ALL MY POWER-- ALL MY STRENGTH-- I COULDN'T SAVE HIM!

7

AS FOR THE REST, BY SOME FANTASTIC STROKE OF FATE, I MUST HAVE BEEN FROZEN IN AN ICE FLOE, AND THEN FOUND BY SOME ESKIMOS WHO THOUGHT I WAS A SUPERNATURAL OBJECT! THEN, ALL THOSE YEARS OF BEING IN A STATE OF FROZEN SUSPENDED ANIMATION MUST HAVE PREVENTED ME FROM AGING!

WE BELIEVE YOU, CAPTAIN AMERICA!

NOT LONG AFTERWARDS, AS THE RED, WHITE AND BLUE-CLAD FIGURE RESTS BELOW FROM HIS GRUELLING ORDEAL...

WE HAVE REACHED OUR DESTINATION! PREPARE FOR MOORING!

SLOW DOWN, GIANT-MAN! I CAN'T MATCH THOSE BIG STRIDES OF YOURS! HMMM, LOOKS LIKE THE GENTLEMEN OF THE PRESS WERE EXPECTING US!

THEY KNOW WE WENT AFTER THE HULK!* THEY EXPECT A BIG STORY!

TOO BAD WE'LL HAVE TO DISAPPOINT THEM! WE HAD A BANG-UP FIGHT, BUT NO REAL RESULTS!

AHH, BUT WAIT TILL THEY LEARN WHO OUR PASSENGER IS, BELOW DECKS!

*SEE THE AVENGERS #3 "THE HULK AND SUB-MARINER"—ED.

THEN SUDDENLY, UNEXPECTEDLY, AT THAT VERY SPLIT-SECOND, A BLINDING FLASH TAKES PLACE--FAR BRIGHTER THAN ANY ORDINARY FLASH-BULB EXPLOSION SHOULD BE!

AND, AFTER THE SMOKE HAS CLEARED, THE AVENGERS SEEM TO BE GONE-- AS IN THEIR PLACE THE CROWD SEES FOUR MOTIONLESS, STONE STATUES!

HEY, PETE-- LOOK! WHAT DO YOU MAKE OF THAT?

AW, PROBABLY SOME KINDA TRICK THE AVENGERS USED TO DUCK OUT OF AN INTERVIEW!

8

BITTERLY DISAPPOINTED, THE REPORTERS AND PHOTOGRAPHERS RUSH OFF, TRYING TO FIND THE AVENGERS... AS THE CROWD DRIFTS AWAY TO NOTHINGNESS...

THAT'S A PRETTY CRUMMY TRICK TO PULL ON US, AFTER US WAITING ALL DAY FOR THIS INTERVIEW!

LET'S GO *FIND* 'EM! THEY COULDN'T HAVE GOTTEN FAR!

MINUTES LATER, THE LAST OCCUPANT OF THE UNDERSEA CRAFT SLOWLY CLIMBS UP THE HATCHWAY, HAVING BEEN AWAKENED BY THE COMMOTION ABOVE...

BUT, UPON REACHING THE SURFACE, HE FINDS...

EVERYONE'S *GONE!* THE PIER IS *DESERTED!* BUT-- WHY WOULD THEY DASH OFF *WITHOUT* ME ??

STRANGE... THOSE STATUES MUST BE IN HONOR OF THE AVENGERS! BUT THEY ARE NOT SCULPTED IN TYPICAL POSES! OH WELL, IT'S NO CONCERN OF MINE! I HAVE A WHOLE NEW WORLD TO REDISCOVER-- A WORLD WHICH HAS ADVANCED TWENTY YEARS AHEAD OF ME!

HMMM, THE GIRLS ARE STILL AS LOVELY AS EVER... BUT THE FASHIONS, THE HAIRDOS,... HOW DIFFERENT THEY ARE!

HOLY SMOKE! THAT *CAN'T* BE WHO I *THINK* IT IS!

SALLY--*LOOK!* HE RESEMBLES A FIGURE I HEARD MY FATHER TALK ABOUT-- A MIGHTY HERO OF YEARS AGO!

OF *COURSE!* MY OLDER BROTHER TOLD ME ABOUT HIM MANY TIMES-- IT WAS *CAPTAIN AMERICA!*

AND THE NEW YORK SKY-LINE--EVER IMPRESSIVE-- EVER CHANGING! WHAT CAN *THIS* MAGNIFICENT STRUCTURE BE-- WITH ALL THE WORLD'S FLAGS ARRAYED AROUND IT ??

HEY! WATCH THE *LIGHTS* CROSSING THE STREET, MAC!

THE CARS HAVE CHANGED MOST OF ALL-- AS THEY ALWAYS DO! WE NEVER HAD SO MANY *SMALL* ONES IN THE THIRTIES AND FORTIES!

WAIT! I KNOW YOU! YOU'RE-- AWW, NO! IT *CAN'T* BE! IT'S *IMPOSSIBLE!*

BUT I *CAN'T* BE WRONG! I *SAW* YOU ONCE, WHEN I WAS A KID! NEVER *FORGOT* IT!

9

I DIDN'T MEAN TO THROW YOU A CURVE BY CALLING YOU BUCKY! YOU SEE, HE-- ONCE WAS A CLOSE FRIEND OF MINE-- BUT HE'S GONE NOW! I WAS WASTING TIME-- MOURNING HIM-- BUT YOU'VE SUDDENLY MADE ME REALIZE THAT LIFE GOES ON! IN A WAY, BUCKY CAN STILL LIVE AGAIN!

LOOK, FELLA-- AFTER WE FIND THE AVENGERS, I'M SURE THEY CAN RECOMMEND A REAL NICE HEAD SHRINKER FOR YOU!

HE THINKS I'M SOME SORT OF MADMAN! WELL, I'LL PROVE TO HIM THAT I'M NOT!

PICTURES WERE TAKEN OF THE AVENGERS AT THE DOCK! GET GOING! I WANT TO STUDY THEM!

SURE, CAP! RIGHT AWAY!

ALL OF A SUDDEN HE'S CHANGED! HE ACTS LIKE A GUY WHO'S USED TO BEING OBEYED -- AND FAST!

MINUTES LATER, IN A DARKROOM BELONGING TO ONE OF RICK'S TEEN-BRIGADE MEMBERS...

THESE NEWS PICTURES SEEM ALRIGHT, BUT I'M NOT SATISFIED! CAN YOU MAKE ENLARGEMENTS?

SURE! THERE'S AN ENLARGER AROUND HERE SOMEWHERE!

AND SO...

IT'LL BE READY IN A MINUTE!

AH! THAT'S MORE LIKE IT! THAT'S WHAT I WANTED!

WHAT IS IT? I DON'T SEE ANYTHING!

WAIT-- IT'S GETTING CLEARER! NOW LOOK!

NO PRESS PHOTOG'S CAMERA EVER LOOKED LIKE THAT-- NOT EVEN TWENTY YEARS LATER!

IT-- IT LOOKS LIKE SOME KINDA GUN!

IT'S UP TO YOU NOW, SON! IF YOU WANT TO LEARN WHAT HAPPENED TO THE AVENGERS, YOU'VE GOT TO FIND THAT MAN IN THE PICTURE!

NOW YOU'RE TALKIN' MY LANGUAGE, CAP! JUST SIT TIGHT AND WATCH MY SMOKE! I'LL ALERT MY TEEN-BRIGADE, ALL OVER THE CITY...

11

WITHIN AN HOUR, THE SEARCH IS ON, AS SHARP-EYED TEEN-AGERS COVER THE CITY, SEEKING A PASTY-FACED MAN, WEARING OVAL SUN-GLASSES, WITH JET BLACK HAIR! NOT MUCH TO GO ON, PERHAPS, BUT STILL A STARTING POINT FOR THE EAGER BRIGADERS...

THAT'S NOT HIM! HAIR'S NOT BLACK ENOUGH!

THOUGHT I HAD HIM-- BUT HE'S MUCH TOO OLD!

WORKING AROUND THE CLOCK, THE ALERT TEEN-BRIGADE TAKES CANDID CAMERA SNAP-SHOTS OF ALL POSSIBLE SUS-PECTS, SENDING THEM IMMEDIATELY TO RICK JONES...

THAT GUY'S ANOTHER FALSE ALARM, BUT I'VE GOT A HALF-DOZEN SNAPS TO SEND RICK ANYWAY!

THEN, RACING THRU THE VAST CITY LIKE AN AVENGING STREAK, THE NIMBLE, SEEMINGLY TIRELESS CAPTAIN AMERICA FOLLOWS UP EACH LEAD, NO MATTER WHERE IT MAY TAKE HIM...

IT'S LIKE OLD TIMES AGAIN, BEING IN COSTUME--ON THE TRAIL OF SOME STRANGE, UNKNOWN MENACE!

THIS IS WHAT I WAS MEANT TO DO! THIS IS THE DESTINY I CAN NEVER ESCAPE!

AND THEN, FINALLY...

IT'S HIM! THE ONE WE'RE AFTER!

WITHOUT A MOMENT'S HESITATION, TWO HUNDRED POUNDS OF FIGHTING FURY CRASH THRU THE SHATTERING WINDOW.

BUT, IN HIS EAGERNESS, THE ATTACKING CRIME-FIGHTER HAS FAILED TO NOTICE THE GUNMEN IN THE ADJOINING ROOM--GUNMEN WHO HEAR THE CRASH AND RACE TO THE SCENE, THEIR WEAPONS THUNDERING!!

GET THAT COSTUMED CLOWN, WHO-EVER HE IS!

IT'LL BE A CINCH!

12

VERY WELL! I SEE THAT FURTHER RESISTANCE IS USELESS!

AFTER YOU HAVE HEARD MY STORY, YOU MAY FEEL *PITY* FOR ME, INSTEAD OF THAT RAW HATRED WHICH I SEE MIRRORED IN YOUR EYES!

I WAS *RIGHT!* YOU'RE *NOT* A HUMAN!

HOLY COW! LOOK WHAT WE'VE BEEN *WORKIN'* FOR! LEMME *OUT* OF HERE!

I'VE *HAD* IT! ME FOR THE STRAIGHT AND *NARROW* FROM NOW ON!

NOW I'LL TELL YOU WHAT *I* THINK! THOSE AREN'T *STATUES* OF THE AVENGERS! THEY ARE THE AVENGERS *THEMSELVES,* TURNED INTO STONE BY YOU, WHEN YOU USED YOUR RAY ON THEM WHILE POSING AS A NEWSPAPER PHOTOGRAPHER! *ADMIT IT!*

YES! YES! YOU'RE RIGHT! UNHAND ME! I CANNOT BEAR PHYSICAL CONTACT WITH PRIMITIVE BEINGS!

"I COME FROM A FAR DISTANT GALAXY! MY NAME WOULD BE MEANINGLESS TO YOU AS EARTH TONGUES CANNOT EVEN PRONOUNCE IT!"

"CENTURIES AGO, DUE TO ENGINE FAILURE, MY SPACE SHIP CRASHED ON EARTH, IMBEDDING ITSELF DEEP INTO THE BOTTOM OF THE SEA!"

"I MEANT EARTHLINGS NO HARM! I ROAMED YOUR PLANET, SEEKING SOMEONE TO HELP ME FREE MY SHIP! BUT THOSE I SAW *FEARED* ME--ATTACKED ME! IN SELF-DEFENSE I USED MY RAY GUN ON THEM, TURNING THEM TO STONE FOR ONE HUNDRED OF YOUR EARTH HOURS.'"

BEHOLD! IT IS A *MONSTER* FROM THE *NETHERWORLD!* IT MUST BE *SLAIN!*

NO! I NEED *HELP!* STAY BACK --PLEASE--DON'T MAKE ME *DO* THIS! *NO!*

IT IS BE-WITCHED! ONE LOOK AT IT TURNS MEN TO *STONE!*

YOUR HAIR-- IN THE DARK, YOU MUST HAVE LOOKED LIKE A *WOMAN* TO THEM--AND TURNING MEN TO STONE--*THAT* MUST BE THE ORIGIN OF THE LEGEND OF *MEDUSA!* BUT--WHY DID YOU USE YOUR POWER ON THE *AVENGERS??*

BECAUSE OF THE ONE WHO CALLS HIMSELF *SUB-MARINER!* HE FOUND ME SOME DAYS AGO--TOLD ME *HE* WOULD FREE MY SHIP FROM THE OCEAN'S DEPTHS IF I WOULD TURN THE AVENGERS TO STONE! I-I *HAD* TO DO IT!

14

87

SUB-MARINER! I SEEM TO REMEMBER THAT NAME FROM THE DIM PAST! BUT TIME ENOUGH FOR HIM LATER! FIRST, YOU MUST BRING THE AVENGERS BACK TO LIFE-- AND WE WILL FREE YOUR SHIP FOR YOU!

IF ONLY YOU MEAN IT! IF ONLY I CAN BELIEVE YOU!

CAPTAIN AMERICA DOES NOT LIE! LET'S GO!

WITHIN MINUTES, THE SWASHBUCKLING ADVENTURER BRINGS THE DEFEATED ALIEN TO A WAREHOUSE WHERE THE "STATUES" HAVE BEEN STORED! THEN, FACING THE MOTIONLESS FIGURES, HE DIRECTS HIS RAY AT THEM AGAIN, AFTER FIRST REVERSING THE POLARITY!

IT'S WORKING! THEY'RE TURNING TO NORMAL!

MEANWHILE, FAR BENEATH THE SURFACE OF THE SEA, IN HIS NOW-DESERTED IMPERIAL CASTLE, A FURIOUS, FRUSTRATED PRINCE NAMOR OBSERVES THE SCENE ABOVE THRU HIS UNDERSEA SCANNER...

MY PLAN HAS FAILED! THE ONE WHO CALLS HIMSELF CAPTAIN AMERICA HAS ROBBED ME OF MY VICTORY!

BUT THIS WILL TEACH ME A LESSON! WHATEVER THE SUB-MARINER MUST DO, HE MUST DO ALONE!

I AM STILL THE MOST POWERFUL MUTANT ON EARTH-- HALF-HUMAN, HALF SEA-CREATURE! MY BRAIN IS AGILE, MY ENERGY INEXHAUSTIBLE! I MUST KEEP STRIKING UNTIL THE AVENGERS ARE DESTROYED!

AND THEN, A FICKLE FATE SEEMS TO SMILE AT NAMOR, AS HE SEES...

A TROOP OF MY ELITE GUARD! THEY HAVE NOT DESERTED ME! THEY ARE STILL SEARCHING FOR ME!

THEY SEE ME-- THEY ARE TURNING! THEY BOW IN LOYAL ACKNOWLEDGEMENT OF MY IMPERIAL PRESENCE! AND NOW-- PRINCE NAMOR IS NO LONGER ALONE!

15

QUICKLY PRESSING A CONCEALED STUD ON HIS CONTROL PANEL, IRON MAN UNLEASHES THE FULL FORCE OF HIS TRANSISTOR-POWERED MAGNETIC REPULSER!

NOW I'VE GOT TO HOPE I CAN THINK OF SOMETHING *FAST!* AT FULL INTENSITY, MY MAGNETIC RAY WILL ONLY LAST ANOTHER FEW SECONDS!

AND, NO SOONER DO THE MINIATURIZED TRANSISTORS LOSE THEIR POWER, THAN THE ENRAGED *NAMOR* CATCHES ONTO A NEARBY BOULDER, AND...

FOOL! YOU HAVE EXHAUSTED YOUR GREATEST WEAPON, WHILE *I* AM STRONGER THAN EVER!

WHILE MY LOYAL WARRIORS PREVENT THE OTHERS FROM COMING TO YOUR AID, I'LL GIVE YOU A SMALL DEMONSTRATION OF MY IMPERIAL MIGHT!

HE SMASHED THAT HUGE BOULDER LIKE AN EGGSHELL! THE FLYING CHUNKS ARE HITTING ME--OHHH--

I'LL DESTROY THE AVENGERS ONE AT A TIME! IT WILL AFFORD ME FAR GREATER SATISFACTION THIS WAY!

I'VE *GOT* TO HOLD OUT JUST A FEW MINUTES LONGER--!

SOON MY TRANSISTORS WILL BUILD UP THEIR POWER PEAK AGAIN, AND THEN I'LL MAKE THAT ARROGANT FISHMAN CHANGE HIS TUNE!!

MEANTIME, THE *WASP* OBSERVES IRON MAN'S DESPERATE PLIGHT, AND...

NAMOR IS *MERCILESS!* I'VE GOT TO HELP! PERHAPS IF I TAKE A CAPSULE AND BECOME WASP-SIZED...

YOU FIGHT VALIANTLY-- FOR A HUMAN! BUT THIS IS YOUR *FINISH!!*

I'LL SMASH YOUR BUILT-IN HAND WEAPONS BEFORE THEY CAN BE USED AGAINST ME AGAIN!

BUT, AT THAT MOMENT, A SMALL, INSISTENT DAZZLING OBJECT FLIES FRANTICALLY AROUND NAMOR'S HEAD, TEMPORARILY BLINDING THE BATTLING SEA MONARCH!

WHAT IS *THIS??* I-I CANNOT *SEE--!*

MY LORD! LEAVE THE MAN OF IRON! COME TO OUR AID, SIRE! WE ARE SORELY BESEIGED!

18

91

MEANWHILE, WHAT OF THE THIRD AVENGER -- AND CAPTAIN AMERICA?? THEY HAD BOTH BEEN HURLED BACK INTO THE SEA BY THE EARTH-SHATTERING BLAST WHICH HERALDED NAMOR'S ATTACK! AND NOW, WE FIND GIANT-MAN AT THE BRINK OF DISASTER...

CAN'T HOLD MY BREATH MUCH LONGER! ONLY ONE CHANCE -- MY REDUCING CAPSULE... THERE! I SWALLOWED IT!

IN THE WINK OF AN EYE, THE DOUBLE-SIZED ADVENTURER BECOMES ANT MAN, AND EASILY SWIMS TO FREEDOM THRU THE NOW LIMP ROPES!

MADE IT! WONDER WHAT HAPPENED TO CAPTAIN AMERICA?? WELL, NO TIME TO SEARCH FOR HIM NOW!

UH OH! MY ANT-SIZE IS FINE FOR ESCAPING FROM ROPES, BUT IF I DON'T WANNA END MY DAYS AS FISH FOOD, I'D BETTER BECOME GIANT-MAN AGAIN -- AND PRONTO!

AND SO... STRANGE... STILL NO SIGN OF CAPTAIN AMERICA! NOR DO I SEE THE SUB-MARINER! I WONDER --??

WAIT! OVER THERE! IRON MAN IS BATTLING AGAINST HEAVY ODDS! PERHAPS I CAN EVEN THEM JUST A BIT!

IF ALL YOU BULLY-BOYS ENJOY GANGING UP ON ONE MAN, TRY ME FOR SIZE! HEY, I NOTICE YOU'RE NOT WHOOPING IT UP SO MUCH NOW!

GO ON BACK TO THE DEPTHS YOU CAME FROM! WE'VE NO QUARREL WITH YOU! IT'S THAT POWER-MAD PRINCE OF YOURS WE'RE AFTER!

93

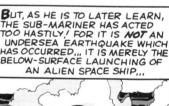

NOT UNTIL LATER WILL THE IRONY OF THE SITUATION DAWN UPON THE FRUSTRATED SEA PRINCE! FOR THE VERY ALIEN HE HAD HOPED WOULD *DESTROY* THE AVENGERS HAS UNWITTINGLY *RESCUED* THEM AT THE CRUCIAL MOMENT!

IT'S THE *ALIEN!* HE'S RETURNING TO THE STARS!

THE WATERS HAVE SUBSIDED! THE ISLAND IS STILL INTACT!

BUT NAMOR IS GONE--AND SO IS OUR CHANCE TO DEFEAT HIM!

EASY, LAD! IT'S ALL OVER! YOU'RE SAFE NOW!

I NOTICE IT TOOK A THREAT TO THE *BOY* TO BRING YOU INTO ACTION, FELLA!

THOUGH NAMOR IS GONE, I FEEL WE SHALL MEET HIM AGAIN--IN MORTAL COMBAT! BUT, ONE OF US IS *STILL* NOT PRESENT!

I THOUGHT YOU'D *NEVER* NOTICE, BLUE-EYES!

I WAS DOING WHAT *ANY* GIRL WOULD DO IN A MOMENT OF CRISIS--POWDERING MY NOSE, OF COURSE!

ONLY *ONE* THING PUZZLES ME --WHEN I WRITE THIS DOWN IN MY DIARY, DO I CALL IT A *VICTORY*-- OR A *DEFEAT??*

THAT'S FOR *HISTORY* TO DECIDE, HON! RIGHT NOW, WE'VE *ANOTHER* DECISION TO AWAIT...

RIGHT, WE HAVE AN *OFFER* TO PROPOSE TO CAPTAIN AMERICA!

I HAVE SEEN YOU IN BATTLE --AND THERE ARE NONE BRAVER! IF YOUR OFFER IS WHAT I *HOPE* IT IS, MY ANSWER IS *YES!*

SPOKEN WITH HONOR, AND WITH DIGNITY, LIKE A *MAN!*

THUS, WE ARE PRIVILEGED TO WITNESS A MOMENTOUS MOMENT IN THE ANNALS OF HIGH ADVENTURE...

WE WELCOME YOU, CAPTAIN AMERICA, TO THE RANKS OF-- *THE AVENGERS!*

23

BUT, THERE IS ONE WHOSE HEART IS STILL HEAVY--STILL FILLED WITH A DREAD FEAR--

HE'S THE GREATEST GUY I EVER MET-- AND I CAN TELL HE WANTS ME TO BE HIS PARTNER! BUT WHAT ABOUT--THE *HULK??*

HE'S SURE TO RETURN *SOME DAY*... AND WHEN HE FINDS OUT THAT *CAPTAIN AMERICA* HAS REPLACED HIM--WILL *ANYTHING* BE ABLE TO STOP HIM THEN??!

BUT, NOTHING IN LIFE IS CERTAIN! AND WE MUST TAKE THE GOOD AND THE BAD AS FATE DEALS THEM OUT! *ONE* THING IS CERTAIN, THOUGH-- NEXT ISSUE OF *THE AVENGERS* WILL HAVE MORE SUPER HEROES, SUPER-VILLAINS, AND SUPER-THRILLS--JUST AS *YOU* WANT THEM!

THE END

THE MIGHTY AVENGERS

"The INVASION of The LAVA MEN!"

ANOTHER EPIC IN THE ANNALS OF THE STRONGEST SUPER-TEAM OF ALL! STARRING: THE MIGHTY THOR, IRON MAN, CAPTAIN AMERICA AND RICK JONES, GIANT-MAN AND THE WONDERFUL WASP!

AN ALL NEW SUPER-SAGA PRODUCED WITH PRIDE BY THE WORLD-FAMOUS MARVEL COMICS GROUP

X·652

AN EPIC TALE TOLD WITH HIGH DRAMA AND HEROIC DIGNITY BY: STAN LEE ILLUSTRATED WITH DEEP SINCERITY AND DAZZLING BEAUTY BY: JACK KIRBY INKED BY: PAUL REINMAN LETTERED BY: S. ROSEN

IN THE UNFORGETTABLE *FANTASTIC FOUR #26*, WE SAW THE SENSATIONAL BATTLE BETWEEN THE *HULK* AND THE *THING*... A BATTLE LATER JOINED BY THE MIGHTY *AVENGERS!* BUT ALL THINGS MUST END AND SO, WITH THE DISAPPEARANCE OF THE HULK, THE AVENGERS RETURN TO THEIR MEETING PLACE TO INSPECT THE DAMAGE...

WELL, THERE'S NOT MUCH MORE WE CAN DO HERE! WE'LL HAVE TO CALL A CONSTRUCTION CREW TO PUT ANTHONY STARK'S HOME IN ORDER AGAIN!

I SUGGEST WE DISBAND FOR NOW! WE ALL HAVE PERSONAL MATTERS TO ATTEND TO!

CONSIDERING THE FIGHT THE HULK PUT UP, IT'S A WONDER THE HOUSE WASN'T DAMAGED EVEN WORSE!

I'M TOO TIRED TO WALK, JAN! LET'S SHRINK DOWN AND I'LL SUMMON MY FLYING ANTS!

YOU'VE GOT IT *MADE*, BIG BOY! YOU RIDE YOUR ANTS, WHILE *I* HAVE TO FLY BY MYSELF!

AS EACH TAKES A SHRINKING CAPSULE, GIANT-MAN AND THE WASP SEEM TO SUDDENLY FADE FROM SIGHT!

WELL, BIG FELLA, IT WAS A GOOD FIGHT WHILE IT LASTED, AND... *HOLY SMOKE!* WHERE'D HE GO?

C'MON, DOLL! I'LL RACE YOU TO THE LAB! START FLAPPIN' THOSE WINGS, HONEY!

AT *LEAST* YOU COULD GIVE YOUR LITTLE WASP A *HEAD START!*

STAND BACK, MY FRIENDS! THE TIME HAS COME FOR MY DEPARTURE!

BUT SHOULD THE NEED ARISE, MY ENCHANTED HAMMER AND MYSELF ARE AT YOUR BECK AND CALL, AS EVER!

NOW TO RETURN TO THE HEART OF THE CITY, AND RESUME MY MORTAL GUISE AS DR. DON BLAKE, PRACTICING PHYSICIAN!

2.

IT WAS A PLEASURE TO FIGHT SHOULDER TO SHOULDER WITH YOU, CAPTAIN AMERICA! WE ARE PROUD TO NUMBER YOU AMONG THE AVENGERS... PROUD THAT YOU CHOSE TO JOIN US!*

I COULD NOT HAVE SELECTED A FINER FIGHTING GROUP! MY SKILL AND MY SHIELD ARE YOURS, WHENEVER YOU NEED THEM! REMEMBER THAT, IRON MAN!

*SEE THE AVENGERS #4 - EDITOR.

SINCE THE HULK TURNED AGAINST US... AND AGAINST HIS OWN ALLY, RICK JONES, IT'S LUCKY THAT THE BOY FOUND A FRIEND LIKE CAPTAIN AMERICA!

REMEMBER THOSE ACROBATIC TRICKS I PROMISED TO TEACH YOU, RICK? THIS IS AS GOOD A TIME AS ANY!

THAT'S GREAT, CAP!

A FINE THING! THE MILLIONAIRE INDUSTRIALIST, TONY STARK, LETS THE AVENGERS USE HIS NEW YORK MANSION FOR THEIR MEETING PLACE... AND I'M THE ONLY ONE LEFT TO FIX THE PLACE UP NOW! WONDER IF THE AVENGERS SUSPECT THAT IRON MAN REALLY IS LOVABLE OL' TONY STARK!?

A FEW DAYS LATER, AT TONY STARK'S WEAPONS FACTORY IN FLUSHING, LONG ISLAND, WHERE A NEW TRANSISTORIZED ARTILLERY COMPUTER IS BEING ASSEMBLED...

THAT'S IT, FRANK! SHE'S ALL SET FOR THE PRELIMINARY TESTING!

RIGHT ON SCHEDULE! MR. STARK WILL BE MIGHTY PLEASED!

SUDDENLY, A STRANGE, PIERCING SOUND FILLS THE FACTORY... A SOUND OF SUCH PULSE-STOPPING INTENSITY THAT IT SEEMS LIKE A LIVING THING!

THAT NOISE! WHAT IS IT?? IT...IT'S ALMOST UNBEARABLE!

WITHIN SECONDS, THE SHRILL VIBRATIONS OF THE HIGH-PITCHED BLAST ACTUALLY CAUSE THE DELICATE PROTOTYPE MACHINE TO FALL APART IN ONE SUDDEN UPHEAVAL!

OH, NO!! THE SOUNDS SEEM TO HAVE RIPPED OUR COMPUTER APART!

MINUTES LATER, A PHONE INSISTENTLY RINGS IN TONY STARK'S PRIVATE APARTMENT!

MY PRIVATE WIRE! MUST BE SOMETHING IMPORTANT!

3.

WHAT?? YOU SAY A MYSTERIOUS NOISE CAUSED ALL THAT DAMAGE?! I'LL BE RIGHT THERE! IN THE MEAN-TIME, ITEMIZE THE COST OF REPLACEMENT AND DON'T TOUCH A THING UNTIL I ARRIVE!

AND THEN, THE MILLIONAIRE PLAYBOY INDUSTRIALIST CONNECTS A CAREFULLY INSULATED WIRE FROM A DEVICE THAT NEVER LEAVES HIS CHEST TO THE NEAREST WALL OUTLET...

HOW IRONIC IT IS! I'M THE ENVY OF MILLIONS, BECAUSE OF MY WEALTH AND MY ALLEGED GOOD LOOKS! THERE'S HARDLY A MAN ON EARTH WHO WOULDN'T WANT TO BE IN MY SHOES!

BUT HOW MANY WOULD STILL FEEL THAT WAY IF THEY KNEW THAT MY LIFE WILL LAST ONLY AS LONG AS THIS CHEST DEVICE KEEPS MY HEART BEATING?! IF THEY KNEW THAT I LIVE EVERY MOMENT WITH THE THREAT OF SUDDEN DEATH DUE TO THE PIECE OF SHRAPNEL LODGED IN MY HEART!

BUT LET US LEAVE TONY STARK ALONE WITH HIS SOBER THOUGHTS, AS WE TURN OUR ATTENTION TO ANT-MAN AND THE WASP, WHO ARE ENGAGED IN A RESEARCH PROJECT DEEP WITHIN A THRIVING ANT HILL...

HAVE YOU FOUND WHAT YOU'RE LOOKING FOR YET, HANK? THIS PLACE IS TOO DRY FOR MY DELICATE COMPLEXION!

JUST A LITTLE LONGER, JAN! I'M INTERESTED IN OBSERVING THE ACTION OF THESE ISOTOPES THAT CANNOT BE STUDIED BY ANY OTHER METHOD!

AND THEN, UNEXPECTEDLY, WITH NERVE-SHATTERING IMPACT, THE SAME MYSTERIOUS SOUND WHICH ROCKED TONY STARK'S FACTORY IS HEARD IN THE DEPTHS OF THE TINY ANT HILL!!

HENRY! THAT SOUND!! WHA... WHAT IS IT?? IT'S THE MOST UNEARTHLY THING I'VE EVER HEARD!!

I DON'T KNOW, JAN!...BUT LOOK HOW IT'S AFFECTING THE ANTS! IT'S DRIVING THEM FROM THE ANT HILL!

JAN! THE VIBRATIONS ARE MAKING THE ENTIRE HILL CAVE IN! WE'VE GOT TO GET OUT! FOLLOW ME!

JUST LEAD THE WAY, BLUE EYES! I'M RIGHT BEHIND YOU!

SECONDS LATER...

WE MADE IT! ARE YOU ALL RIGHT, HONEY?

I'M AS ALL RIGHT AS ANY GIRL COULD BE WHO HAD ALL HER MAKE-UP SMUDGED BY A SILLY OL' COLLAPSING ANT HILL!

NEVER MIND THAT, JAN! OUR BIG PROBLEM IS TO LEARN THE SECRET OF THAT STRANGE SOUND!

4.

A SHORT TIME LATER, IN THE MEDICAL OFFICE OF DR. DON BLAKE...

I BROUGHT YOU YOUR LUNCH AND A NEWSPAPER, DOCTOR! YOU'VE JUST *GOT* TO TAKE TIME OUT FOR YOUR MEALS!

NOW, JANE...WOULD YOU LOVE ME AS MUCH IF I WERE FAT AND GLUTTONOUS?

DOCTOR BLAKE! WHO EVER TOLD YOU I LOVE YOU?

JUST A JOKE, DEAR! *SAY!* LOOK AT THIS! *ANOTHER* DISASTER ASSOCIATED WITH A MYSTERIOUS SUDDEN SOUND!! IT SEEMS TO BE HAPPENING ALL OVER THE COUNTRY!

Daily Record-Ledger

NEW TRAIN ACCIDENT! ENGINEER CLAIMS A MYSTERIOUS SOUND CAUSED HIM TO LOSE CONTROL!

NO CASUALTIES AS FREIGHT TRAIN JUMPS TRACK IN

THEN, AS SOON AS HIS NURSE HAS RETURNED TO THE OUTER OFFICE, THE SLENDER, LAME DOCTOR RUSHES TO THE ROOF OF HIS BUILDING...

THERE CAN BE NO FURTHER DELAY! IT IS TIME TO SUMMON THE *AVENGERS!!*

BUT I CANNOT SUMMON THE STRONGEST TEAM OF SUPER HEROES ON EARTH IN THE IDENTITY OF DON BLAKE!

AND SO, WITH ONE STRIKE OF MY CANE UPON THE SURFACE BENEATH, I AM TRANSFORMED TO THE MIGHTY *THOR!!*

BUT ONCE AGAIN WE SHIFT OUR SCENE---THIS TIME TO ANOTHER ROOFTOP, WHERE WE FIND THE COLORFUL *CAPTAIN AMERICA* GIVING AN ACROBATIC EXHIBITION TO RICK JONES AND MEMBERS OF HIS TEEN BRIGADE ...

AND NOW I'LL SHOW YOU *WHY* IT'S SO VITALLY IMPORTANT TO EAT THE RIGHT FOODS AND GET PLENTY OF EXERCISE AND EIGHT HOURS OF SLEEP!

WHAT'S HE GONNA DO *NOW?*

I DON'T KNOW! ...BUT I BET IT'LL BE A *DOOZY!*

CAN YOU IMAGINE TRYING A STUNT LIKE *THIS* WHEN YOUR LIFE MAY DEPEND ON IT IF YOU'RE NOT IN PEAK CONDITION?

HOLY HANNAH! CAP MUST HAVE SOME KINDA *FLYING BELT* UNDER HIS SHIRT!

DON'T KID YOUR- SELF! EVEN A FLYING BELT COULDN'T DO WHAT THAT GUY'S TRAINED *MUSCLES* CAN DO!

5.

103

A SHORT TIME LATER, WHILE THE UPPER PORTION OF HIS EAST SIDE MANSION IS BEING REPAIRED, THE *AVENGERS* HOLD THEIR EMERGENCY MEETING IN THE LUXURIOUS BASEMENT OF ANTHONY STARK'S TOWN HOUSE...

FOCUS THE PROJECTOR ON THE SOUTHWESTERN PORTION OF THE COUNTRY, THOR! *THAT'S* WHERE ALL THE TESTS SHOW THAT THE STRANGE SOUNDS ARE ORIGINATING FROM!

THE SOUTHWEST, EH? ISN'T THAT THE *HULK'S* STAMPING GROUNDS! I WONDER...

NOT A CHANCE, GIANT-MAN! THAT ISN'T THE WAY THE *HULK* OPERATES!

AT THAT VERY MOMENT, AT A HEAVILY GUARDED MISSILE INSTALLATION IN THE VERY PART OF THE COUNTRY WHICH THE AVENGERS ARE DISCUSSING...

HOLY HANNAH! WHAT'S *THAT*?!

I DON'T KNOW! FIRST THAT STRANGE NOISE, AND NOW... A HILL SEEMS TO BE GROWING RIGHT OUT FROM UNDER OUR FEET!

GENERAL ROSS! THERE SEEMS TO BE A DISTURBANCE IN SECTOR THREE, SIR!

DISTURBANCE! IT'S MORE THAN *THAT!* THERE'S A GOL-DURNED *MOUNTAIN* POPPING UP RIGHT NEAR MY LAUNCHING SITE!! GET *RID* OF IT!

Y-YES, SIR! BUT HOW DO YOU GET RID OF A *MOUNTAIN*?!

WHAT *CAUSED* IT IN THE FIRST PLACE??

SUDDENLY, AN INTERRUPTION OCCURS AS GENERAL "THUNDERBOLT" ROSS'S DAUGHTER, BETTY, APPROACHES WITH A SLIM, TENSE-LOOKING YOUNG MAN...

DAD! LOOK WHO I FOUND! IT'S *BRUCE BANNER!* HE'S COME *BACK!*

BANNER! I DIDN'T THINK YOU'D HAVE THE NERVE TO SHOW YOUR FACE HERE AFTER THE WAY YOU DISAPPEARED MONTHS AGO IN THE MIDDLE OF A VITAL ATOMIC TEST!

IF YOU WERE UNDER *MY* COMMAND, INSTEAD OF BEING A CIVILIAN SCIENTIST, I'D SLAP YOU IN THE GUARDHOUSE AS SOON AS *LOOK* AT YOU! WHAT MY DAUGHTER CAN SEE IN A WEAK-KNEED, LILY-LIVERED MILKSOP LIKE YOU...!!!

DAD, *PLEASE!* BRUCE SAID HE'S BEEN *ILL!* THAT'S WHY WE HAVEN'T SEEN HIM! BUT HE'S BETTER NOW!

WELL, WE'LL FINISH DISCUSSING *BANNER* SOME OTHER TIME! RIGHT NOW, I'VE GOT A MORE *IMPORTANT* PROBLEM ON MY HANDS!! *LOOK!* LOOK AT THAT.. THAT MOVING HILL GROWING FROM OUT OF NOWHERE... RIGHT NEAR MY LAUNCHING SITE!!

AND, AS THE RAGING OFFICER TURNS AWAY, BRUCE BANNER REMAINS TRANSFIXED TO THE SPOT, LOST IN HIS OWN STRANGE THOUGHTS...

IF HE THINKS *THAT'S* A PROBLEM, I WONDER WHAT HE'D SAY IF HE KNEW ABOUT *MINE*?? IF HE KNEW THAT DR. BRUCE BANNER IS REALLY...THE *HULK*!!

7.

"CAN I EVER FORGET THAT AWESOME MOMENT, MANY MONTHS AGO, WHEN I WAS STRUCK BY MY OWN *GAMMA RAY BOMB* WHILE TRYING TO SAVE THE LIFE OF RICK JONES, A BOY WHO HAD WANDERED ONTO THE POST DURING THE BOMB TEST..."

"BY SOME MIRACULOUS QUIRK OF FATE, THE GAMMA RAYS DIDN'T KILL ME... ALTHOUGH IT MIGHT HAVE BEEN BETTER IF THEY *HAD!* INSTEAD, THEY CHANGED ME... TURNED ME INTO THE UNBELIEVABLY POWERFUL *HULK!*"

I'LL STAY *WITH* HULK! I'LL NEVER FORGET THAT YOU SAVED MY LIFE!

"AS THE HULK, MY STRENGTH IS VIRTUALLY *LIMITLESS!* EVEN MY LEG MUSCLES ARE SO POWERFUL THAT BY MERELY LEAPING INTO THE AIR, I CAN JUMP VAST DISTANCES, AS THOUGH I'M FLYING!"

"BUT, WITH MY BRUTISH STRENGTH, THERE IS YET *ANOTHER* CHANGE!! MY *PERSONALITY* CHANGES, TOO! THE HULK WANTS TO FIGHT, TO LASH OUT AT THE WORLD THAT DOESN'T UNDERSTAND HIM! AS THE HULK, I BECOME A *MENACE*, EVEN SEEKING TO HARM THE *AVENGERS*, WHO HAVE TRIED TO MAKE ME THEIR ALLY!"

I'VE BECOME A MODERN DAY *JEKYLL AND HYDE!* I CHANGE FROM BANNER TO THE HULK, NEVER KNOWING WHEN THE NEXT CHANGE WILL TAKE PLACE... NEVER DARING TO... HUH?

STOP DAYDREAMING AND MAKE YOURSELF USEFUL, BANNER! YOU'RE A SCIENTIST! WHAT DO *YOU* MAKE OF THAT CONFOUNDED GROWING HILL???

OH, BRUCE... PLEASE TRY TO SOLVE THE MYSTERY FOR MY FATHER! PERHAPS IT WILL MAKE HIM FEEL DIFFERENTLY ABOUT YOU... ABOUT *US!*

I'LL TRY, BETTY! BUT I DON'T KNOW WHAT I CAN DO! I-I'M STILL A LITTLE CONFUSED!

THIS IS *MORE* THAN JUST A SIMPLE HILL! IT SEEMS TO BE COMPOSED OF A TYPE OF SUBSTANCE I'VE NEVER *SEEN* BEFORE! IT LOOKS AS THOUGH IT'S BEING PUSHED UP FROM THE GROUND BY SOME MIGHTY FORCE!

8.

AND, DR. BRUCE BANNER IS CLOSER TO THE TRUTH THAN HE SUSPECTS! FOR, DIRECTLY UNDER THE FEET OF THE MYSTIFIED HUMANS, A FANTASTIC TABLEAU IS TAKING PLACE...

IT'S *WORKING!* AS WE TURN THE GIGANTIC GEARS THAT WE'VE PLACED IN POSITION, THEY ARE PUSHING THE *LIVING ROCK* THROUGH THE CRUST OF EARTH, ONTO THE SURFACE WORLD!

THUS THE SURFACE MEN WILL BE MENACED BY THE DANGER OF THE LIVING ROCK, AND *WE* SHALL BE SAVED!

CONTINUE LIFTING THE *ROCK!* DO NOT STOP UNTIL IT IS ALL *ABOVE* GROUND!

YOUR MAJESTY, LISTEN TO ME! WE MUST NOT *DO* THIS TERRIBLE THING! I ALONE, OF ALL THE LAVA MEN, HAVE *SEEN* THE SURFACE PEOPLE!* THEY ARE NOT EVIL! THEY DO NOT *DESERVE* THIS!

*SEE JOURNEY INTO MYSTERY #97 "THOR VS. THE LAVA MAN!"

SILENCE, MOLTO! NONE MAY SPEAK TO HIS MAJESTY THAT WAY WHILE *I,* HIS LOYAL WITCH DOCTOR, LIVE!

"LOYAL WITCH DOCTOR"!! YOU DO NOT FOOL *ME!* ALL YOU WANT IS A *WAR* BETWEEN US AND THE SURFACE PEOPLE!!

9.

107

108

THEN, THE DETERMINED KING ISSUES A MOMENTOUS COMMAND TO HIS SUBTERRANEAN FORCES...

THE TIME HAS COME! TO THE SURFACE! ATTACK!!

THE OPENING IS BEFORE US! I CAN SEE THE LIGHT OF DAY! AFTER ALL THESE CENTURIES.!!

THE SURFACE SHALL BE OURS! NOTHING CAN STOP US!!

BUT SUDDENLY, A DRAMATIC RED AND GOLD FIGURE APPEARS BETWEEN THE LAVA MEN AND THE SURFACE!

MY TRANSISTORS ARE WEAKENED FROM THE LAST BLAST, BUT I CAN STILL CREATE SOME DUST CLOUDS TO BLIND THEM TEMPORARILY!

HE IS ALONE! HE CANNOT STOP US! DESTROY HIM!

WAIT! I WANT TO TALK TO YOU! YOU'RE JUST A HANDFUL OF UNARMED INVADERS! YOU DON'T KNOW WHAT YOU'LL BE FACING UP ABOVE!

FOOL! WE KNOW ONLY TOO WELL! BUT YOU DO NOT SUSPECT OUR POWERS! SUCH AS THE WAY I CAN HEAT YOUR METAL SUIT UNTIL YOU CAN NO LONGER ENDURE IT!

HE'S RIGHT! TH-THE HEAT IS UNBEARABLE!!

BUT, AT THAT SPLIT SECOND, THE UNDERGROUND CAVERN IS ROCKED BY A BLAST OF ALMOST UNLIMITED POWER!!

AND, WHEN THE SMOKE HAS CLEARED...

EASY, FELLA! YOU'RE OKAY NOW! WE HAD A HUNCH YOU'D BE NEEDIN' US!

NO LIVING BEING, WHETHER ON THE SURFACE OR BELOW IT, MAY ATTACK AN AVENGER WITHOUT ANSWERING TO THE THUNDEROUS HAMMER OF THOR FOR SUCH AN ACT!

12.

"AS A RESULT OF THE TITANIC BLAST, WE FOUND ONE SMALL, STRANGE PIECE OF ROCK! IN AN EFFORT TO DETERMINE WHAT IT WAS, WE STRUCK IT WITH ONE OF OUR TOOLS...

STAND BACK WHILE I SMASH IT!

"ALAS, WE LEARNED TO OUR DISMAY THAT ANY IMPACT CAUSED A VIOLENT EXPLOSION! JUST THE SPEEDING SOUND WAVE THAT RESULTED CAUSED AN ENTIRE DESERTED ISLE IN YOUR PACIFIC OCEAN TO BE BLOWN TO BITS!!

"SINCE THAT DREAD DAY, THE REMAINING FRAGMENT HAS GROWN AND GROWN! IF IT SHOULD EXPLODE NOW, IN ITS PRESENT SIZE, IT COULD SHATTER THE ENTIRE PLANET, DESTROYING BOTH OUR RACES!"

SO, WE HAVE DECIDED ON THE ONLY SOLUTION! WE WILL FORCE IT TO THE SURFACE OF EARTH, WHERE, WHEN IT FINALLY EXPLODES, IT WILL WIPE OUT THOSE WHO DWELL ABOVE US! BUT THE REST OF THE IMPACT WILL GO UP, TOWARD THE SKIES, NOT HARMING THE LAVA MEN! THEN WE SHALL COME TO THE SURFACE AND TAKE OVER WHATEVER REMAINS OF YOUR ONCE-PROUD CIVILIZATION!

BY ASGARD! I DARE NOT STRIKE THE LIVING ROCK... BUT THERE MUST BE SOME WAY TO SAVE MANKIND!

THERE IS NO WAY! YOU HAVE BEATEN US ONCE BEFORE, BUT THIS TIME VICTORY IS OURS! ATTENTION, MEN OF THE LAVA WORLD! THE TIME HAS COME! WE STRIKE FOR VICTORY!

HEARING THE MERCILESS WITCH DOCTOR'S FRENZIED SHOUT, THE ANXIOUS SQUAD OF LAVA MEN RUSH TOWARD THE SURFACE TO ACT AS AN ADVANCE GUARD FOR THE ARMY THAT WILL FOLLOW! BUT, IN THE MOUTH OF THE TUNNEL, THEY FIND...

A SURFACE MAN! BLOCKING OUR PATH! DESTROY HIM!

THAT'LL BE EASIER SAID THAN DONE, FELLA! THIS IS CAPTAIN AMERICA YOU'RE TALKING TO!

WOW! AT A GESTURE, THEY TURNED THE GROUND BENEATH MY FEET TO MOLTEN LAVA!

WELL, IF I CAN'T STAND ON IT, I CAN ALWAYS JUMP OVER IT... AND SEE WHAT HAPPENS NEXT!

15.

LANDING SAFELY IN FRONT OF THE MOLTEN AREA, THE HANDSOME, COSTUMED CAVALIER HOLDS THE LAVA MEN AT BAY WITH HIS WHIRLING SHIELD!

THIS IS A FAR CRY FROM THOR'S *HAMMER*, BUT IT COMES IN HANDY AT A TIME LIKE THIS!

BACK! STAY *BACK!* HIS SHINY SPINNING DISC IS *EVERY-WHERE*... AS IF IT HAS A LIFE OF ITS OWN!!

CLANG!

THAT GAVE THEM SOMETHING TO THINK ABOUT! GLAD I'M NOT TOO RUSTY AFTER ALL THESE YEARS! AND NOW...

QUICKLY! BEFORE HE CAN UNLEASH HIS SHIELD AGAIN! *CINDERIZE HIM!*

"CINDERIZE" ME?? WHA... *HEY!* THEY'VE ACTUALLY HEATED THE AIR AROUND ME! IT'S BECOMING... *SOLIDIFIED*... LIKE A BAND OF UNBREAKABLE CINDERS! HERE COMES *IRON MAN*... AND RICK!

CAREFUL!! THE LAVA MEN ARE MORE POWERFUL THAN WE THOUGHT!

DON'T WORRY ABOUT *THEM*, CAP! THE *AVENGERS* ARE REALLY GETTING INTO HIGH GEAR NOW! WE'LL HAVE YOU FREE BEFORE YOU KNOW IT!!

UGH! THIS STUFF IS STRONGER THAN IT LOOKS! AND I HEAR THE *LAVA MEN* CHARGING TOWARDS US!

STAY WITH CAP, RICKY! *I'LL* HOLD THEM OFF FOR AS LONG AS POSSIBLE!!

TO THE SURFACE!! DEATH TO THE HUMANS!

16.

MEANTIME, DIRECTLY ABOVE, AS GENERAL "THUNDER-BOLT" ROSS'S MISSILES RING THE LIVING STONE, ANT-MAN AND THE WASP MINUTELY EXAMINE EVERY INCH OF ITS SLOWLY-GROWING SURFACE...

I'VE FOUND IT! ONE SMALL AREA THAT ISN'T PULSATING! IF A STRONG ENOUGH BLOW COULD STRIKE THIS EXACT SPOT, IT WOULD DESTROY THE ROCK WITHOUT CAUSING A CATACLYSMIC EXPLOSION!

INSTANTLY, THE ANT-SIZED ADVENTURER BECOMES GIANT-MAN, AND THEN...

LET'S GO, WASP! WE'VE GOT TO FIND THOR! ONLY HIS HAMMER HAS THE POWER WE NEED!

I'LL REMAIN WASP-SIZED SO I CAN KEEP UP WITH YOU BY FLYING!

SECONDS LATER...

WHERE'S THOR? WE NEED HIM TO DEMOLISH THE LIVING STONE!

WE'LL HAVE TO GET PAST THE LAVA MEN FIRST! HE'S ON THE OTHER SIDE OF THEM!

C'MON, GIANT-MAN! I CAN'T HOLD THEM BACK FOREVER! MY TRANSISTORS ARE RUNNING DOWN AGAIN!

THEY'RE STARTING TO MELT THE BOULDER I'M USING! HEY! YOU...YOU'RE NOT RUNNING OUT ON ME?!!

BUT THE TOWERING TITAN HAS ONLY RACED TO THE SURFACE LONG ENOUGH TO SEIZE THE AVENGERS' HELICOPTER! THEN, AIDED BY ITS SPINNING ROTARY BLADE, HE LIFTS THE CRAFT OFF THE GROUND, AND...

STEP ASIDE, IRON MAN! YOU'VE DONE YOUR SHARE! NOW I'LL COOL 'EM OFF FOR YOU!!

17.

114

MEANWHILE, BACK ON THE SURFACE, BRUCE BANNER ALSO HAS JUST SOLVED THE MYSTERY OF THE LIVING ROCK...

IT SENDS SOUND WAVES OVER VAST DISTANCES, REACTING LIKE BOMB BLASTS WHERE THEY LAND! IT WILL EVENTUALLY BLOW ITSELF UP, TAKING HALF THE PLANET *WITH* IT!!

IT WAS PROBABLY CAUSED BY SOME STRANGE UNDERGROUND UPHEAVAL WHICH...

WHA...? I'M...I'M *CHANGING!* IT'S HAPPENING AGAIN! I CAN FEEL IT! *NO!!* DON'T LET IT! I MUSTN'T! NOT NOW!

BUT, ONCE THE INCREDIBLE CHANGE BEGINS TO OCCUR TO BRUCE BANNER'S GAMMA-RAY AFFECTED BODY, NOTHING ON EARTH CAN STOP IT! NOTHING ON EARTH CAN PREVENT HIM FROM BECOMING... *THE HULK!!*

WHAT AM I *DOING* HERE?? WHY DID I... *WAIT!* THAT STRANGE HILL...IT'S SLOWLY GETTING LARGER !! AND I HEAR *VOICES* BELOW...THE VOICES OF... *MY ENEMIES!!*

...SO WE CAN'T STRIKE THE LIVING STONE WITH A MISSILE, OR A POWER HAMMER, OR ANYTHING MAN-MADE, BECAUSE IT WOULD SHATTER TOO LARGE AN AREA, CAUSING IT TO EXPLODE! ONLY YOUR HAMMER CAN HIT THE EXACT SPOT, THOR!

BUT SUDDENLY, THE KEEN EARS OF CAPTAIN AMERICA HEAR THE SOUND OF HEAVY BREATHING, AND...

HOLD IT!! LOOK... BEHIND US!! IT'S *HIM* AGAIN! IT'S... THE *HULK!!*

WE'VE GOT TO GET *RID* OF HIM!

THERE'S NO TIME TO EXPLAIN! THAT LIVING STONE MAY DETONATE ITSELF AT ANY MINUTE!

I'LL SMASH YOU *ALL!* I'LL FINISH WHAT I STARTED LAST TIME WE MET!

HOLD HIM! DON'T LET HIM GO!

19.

WE HAVEN'T TIME TO WASTE ON THE HULK NOW! *FALL BACK,* ALL OF YOU! MY *HAMMER* WILL STOP HIM UNTIL WE'VE ERASED THE DANGER OF THE LIVING STONE!

BUT, AS MIGHTY THOR SWINGS HIS AWESOME HAMMER, THE LAVA MAN *WITCH DOCTOR* STEALS UP BEHIND HIM, HOLDING THE MYSTERIOUS ROD WHICH IS THE SYMBOL OF HIS POWER!

MY RADIOACTIVE ROD AGAINST YOUR WHIRLING HAMMER! LET US *SEE* WHICH IS THE STRONGER!

NOTHING...NOT EVEN AN ATOMIC BLAST...CAN INJURE *THOR* OR HIS ENCHANTED HAMMER...BUT THE POWER RELEASED BY THE GLOWING ROD CAUSES A NUCLEAR SHOCK WAVE!! AND THEN, IN A FREAK, ONE-IN-A-MILLION COMBINATION OF MOLECULES...THE SHOCK WAVE SERVES AS THE CATALYTIC FORCE THAT TRANSFORMS THOR INTO DON BLAKE AGAIN!!

BUT, THE TREMENDOUS IMPACT *ALSO* CAUSES A THUNDEROUS *CAVE-IN,* AS TONS OF ROCK SEPARATE DON BLAKE FROM THE AVENGERS OUTSIDE!!

YOUR POWER IS FAR STRONGER THAN MINE! YOU HAVE MAGICALLY CHANGED INTO ANOTHER BEING! YOU ARE BE-WITCHED!

AND, AS THE WITCH DOCTOR FLEES IN MUTE PANIC, THE WEAKENED FORM OF DR. BLAKE SLUMPS AGAINST THE FALLEN ROCKS, TOO WEAK EVEN TO RAISE HIS CANE...

MUST REST...MUST CLOSE MY EYES...STRAIN WAS TOO GREAT...ONLY THOR'S GREAT STRENGTH LET ME SURVIVE THE ORDEAL!

WHILE, ON THE SURFACE, THE LIVING ROCK ALMOST REACHES ITS MAXIMUM SIZE...

IT'LL EXPLODE ANY MINUTE! AND WITHOUT *THOR,* WE CAN'T DESTROY IT FIRST!

IT WAS *CAPTAIN AMERICA'S* IDEA! IT'S A LONG CHANCE.. BUT IT MIGHT WORK!

STAY BACK! THE WASP AND I HAVE A PLAN!

THAT'S *IT!* LET THE HULK CLIMB A BIT FURTHER! *NOW...NOW* IS THE TIME!

20.

118

AND, THOUGH HIS MORTAL FLESH IS WEAK, HIS *SPIRIT*...HIS *IRON WILL*...ARE STILL THOSE OF THE MIGHTY THUNDER GOD, AND SO...

I'VE *DONE* IT!!

NOW TO BE SURE THE LAVA MEN NEVER AGAIN MENACE THE SURFACE WORLD!

HEAR THE WORDS OF *THOR*, MEN OF THE NETHERWORLD! THE SURFACE MEN ARE NOT YOUR ENEMIES! THEY ONLY DESIRE TO LIVE IN PEACE! BUT, IF YOU EVER AGAIN THREATEN THEIR EXISTENCE, THEY WILL FIGHT TO THE END WITH WEAPONS OF MORE POWER THAN YOU CAN IMAGINE... AND WITH THE *AVENGERS* AT THEIR SIDE!!

NOW RETURN TO YOUR HOMES, TO YOUR NORMAL LIVES! FOR OUR MERCY IS THE EQUAL OF OUR STRENGTH!

IT IS OVER! THE THREAT OF THE LAVA MEN IS ENDED! NOW, IF ONLY THE OTHERS HAVE BEEN ABLE TO DESTROY THE LIVING STONE ...

AND, BACK ON THE SURFACE ...

ORDER THE MISSILES REMOVED FROM STANDBY ALERT, MAJOR! THE DANGER IS OVER!

YES, SIR, GENERAL! LOOKS LIKE THE *AVENGERS* PREVENTED A SHOOTING WAR!

BUT WHAT HAPPENED TO *BRUCE BANNER?* THE LAST I SAW, HE WAS INSPECTING THE LIVING STONE!

GET THOSE MEN BACK TO THEIR STATIONS! NOTIFY THE PENTAGON THE EMERGENCY IS OVER! LOOK ALIVE THERE!

I'VE GOT TO *FIND* BRUCE! THE *HULK* HAS DISAPPEARED! IF THEY SHOULD RUN INTO EACH OTHER, *ANYTHING* MIGHT HAPPEN.!!

MEANWHILE, ON THE SITE WHERE THE LIVING STONE HAD BEEN BUT SECONDS BEFORE ...

THE HULK IS GONE! BUT WE'RE ALL SAFE!

IT'S AMAZING! THE FORCE OF THE GREAT IMPLOSION TRANSMUTED THE GROUND BELOW US INTO A SHEET OF *GLASS!*

WELL, THAT WRAPS IT UP! FUNNY...IT'S ALWAYS SOMEWHAT OF A *LET-DOWN* WHEN A BATTLE IS OVER!

I SUSPECT THIS BATTLE ISN'T *FULLY* ENDED! THE *HULK* ESCAPED DURING THE IMPLOSION ... BUT WE'RE SURE TO MEET HIM *AGAIN!*

SAY! WHAT ABOUT *THOR?* WHERE *IS* HE?

22.

harassed heroes. But powerful as he was, our typewriter was more powerful and we figured out a way to—but, hey, you'll soon see it for yourself.

Our third Avengers classic pits Prince Namor, the legendary Sub-Mariner, against our fabulous fivesome and, to make matters even more explosive, our rampaging green goliath turns upon his former allies and teams up with the Lord of Atlantis! Then, before you have time to catch your breath, you'll discover issue #4, which has become one of the most sought-after collectors' items of all, because it re-introduces one of comicdom's greatest heroes—the sensational, shield-slinging sentinel of liberty who had been frozen in a glacier for

"What a terrific asset the fighting prowess of Captain America would prove to be."

a couple of decades—none other than the charismatic, crowd-pleasing Captain America himself! It was tough to come up with anything that could top that issue, so we didn't even try. Instead, for #5, we went another route and tossed the Lava Men at you, giving us a chance to demonstrate what a terrific asset the fighting prowess of Captain America would prove to be to the mounting popularity of The Avengers.

But let's talk about Cap for a moment. The reason I wanted him to become an Avenger was that I felt he would be the perfect leader. Actually, in the matter of sheer super power, he has less to offer than any of the others. But that's what always intrigued me about ol' wing-head. Despite the fact that he doesn't fly, can't lift a Cadillac with one hand, doesn't shoot power blasts from his fingertips, and has no special power other than his own superb fighting skills and his awesome ability to hurl his red-white-and-blue shield, it seems to me that Steve Rogers always represented the best qualities of America—loyalty, fairness, and courage! It's not too hard for a super-powered Hulk to tackle a few menacing baddies—he knows there's not much chance of him being hurt! But when Cap plunges into battle, he has nothing but his own combat-honed ability to save him!

Another point I should mention: We've always tried to stress characterization here in the hallowed halls of Marvel. We've tried to make our rugged little repertory company as realistic and as true-to-life as possible. In Cap's case, how would someone act, feel, and think who had awakened after being comatose for two decades? It was a challenge to write him so that everything he said and did would be believable to you, the reader. How well we succeeded will be for you to judge—but try to be kind, okay?

From a sales standpoint, team books are always a good idea. Readers seem to love them. But from a creative viewpoint, they're really cool to write. You see, the more characters we have together in a story, the more interplay we can get between them; the more they can argue, kid around, display jealousy, envy, anger, affection and every other emotion. A team is usually a scriptwriter's dream, and a team like the Avengers, ever changing, ever striving, ever growing, is truly a team for all seasons—and all reasons!

Hope you enjoy them as much as I do!

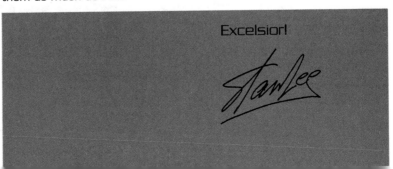

Excelsior!

Stan Lee

INTRODUCTION
by Stan Lee

Questions! Questions! Questions!

Ever since The Avengers' Thirtieth Anniversary took the comic book world by storm, we tireless toilers in the ribald ranks of Marveldom have had a special few urgent questions tossed at us by frantic fans at conventions and comic book stores all around the country.

What better place to answer those burning questions on the lips of Avengerites everywhere than here, on the very pages of this fantastic edition which chronicles the way it all began!

Perhaps the most frequently asked question is, "Way back then, in 1963, why did you decide to take some of Marvel's greatest heroes and put them into a team? And while you're at it, how did you decide which of your heroes would join the team and which you'd leave out, letting them remain as loners?"

> **"One of our biggest problems was finding villains powerful enough to give our titanic team a tussle."**

Of course, it's hard to remember exactly what was in our minds in those early days of Marvel's circuitous climb to glory, but as well as I can recall, here's the straight scoop...

Our other team book, The Fantastic Four, had proven to be one of fandom's most popular, best-selling comics, actually justifying its somewhat boastful subtitle, "The World's Greatest Comic Magazine!" Everywhere we went, readers would ask why we didn't bring out another team of super-powered heroes similar to the popular FF.

Well, you know us. Your wishes are our commands. But we didn't want to simply copy the format of The Fantastic Four. We wanted to try something different, something more unique. Then it hit us. Why not bring together the most oddly assorted group of costumed cavorters imaginable? Take a handful of heroes and heroines who were totally incompatible, completely different, with absolutely nothing in common—except a burning desire to fight for freedom, justice and the chance to star in a Marvel Masterwork—put them together, and see what happens!

We did. And what happened is now history. As you'll see in a moment or two when I get out of your face and let you start reading the really good stuff, we took a hammer-wielding Thunder God, an industrialist in a suit of invincible armor, a green-skinned man-monster, a man and woman who seemed like any ordinary loving couple except for their one rather odd ability of being able to transform themselves to the size of an ant and a wasp, and then we matched this ill-assorted gaggle of good guys against the virtually limitless power of Loki, arguably the most evil being in all the cosmos! And you know something? It worked!

Of course, as you can imagine, one of our biggest problems was finding villains powerful enough to give our titanic team a tussle. In issue #2 you'll meet the Space Phantom, who seemed to have the ability to defeat an entire planet, let alone a group of five

CONTENTS

CREDITS

written by
Stan Lee

penciled by
Jack Kirby

inked by
Dick Ayers
Paul Reinman
George Roussos

colored by
Janet Jackson

lettered by
Sam Rosen
Art Simek

publication design
Joe Kaufman

original series editor
Stan Lee

assistant editor
Mindy Newell

editor
Tom Brevoort

editor in chief
Tom DeFalco

AVENGERS MASTERWORKS™ Originally published in magazine form as AVENGERS #1-5. Published by Marvel Comics, 387 Park Avenue South, New York, N.Y. 10016. Copyright © 1963, 1964, 1993 Marvel Entertainment Group, Inc. All rights reserved. AVENGERS MASTERWORKS and all prominent characters appearing herein and the distinctive likenesses thereof are trademarks of Marvel Entertainment Group, Inc. No part of this book may be printed or reproduced in any manner without the written permission of the publisher. Printed in the United States of America. First Printing: October 1993.
ISBN #0-87135-983-9   GST #R127032852
10 9 8 7 6 5 4 3 2

AVENGERS
MASTERWORKS

VOLUME 1

AVENGERS Nos. 1-5

STAN LEE Ⓐ JACK KIRBY